POKÉMON™

MEET THE POKÉMON OF HOENN

viz media

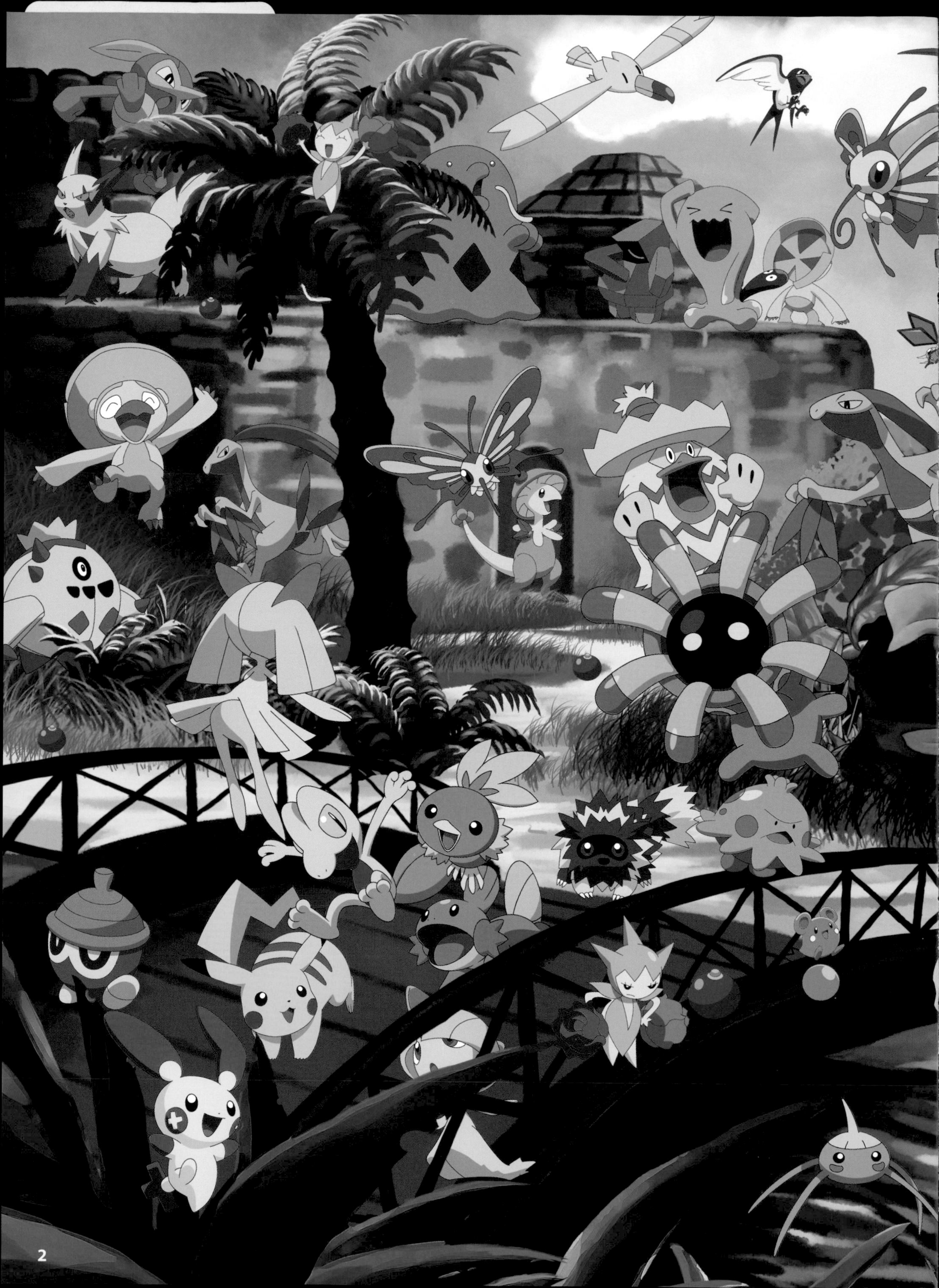

WELCOME TO HOENN!

Mudkip, Treecko, and Torchic join Pikachu for a journey through the beautiful Hoenn region. Let the adventure begin!

LOOK FOR...

×5

×2

Lotad

Roselia

Grovyle

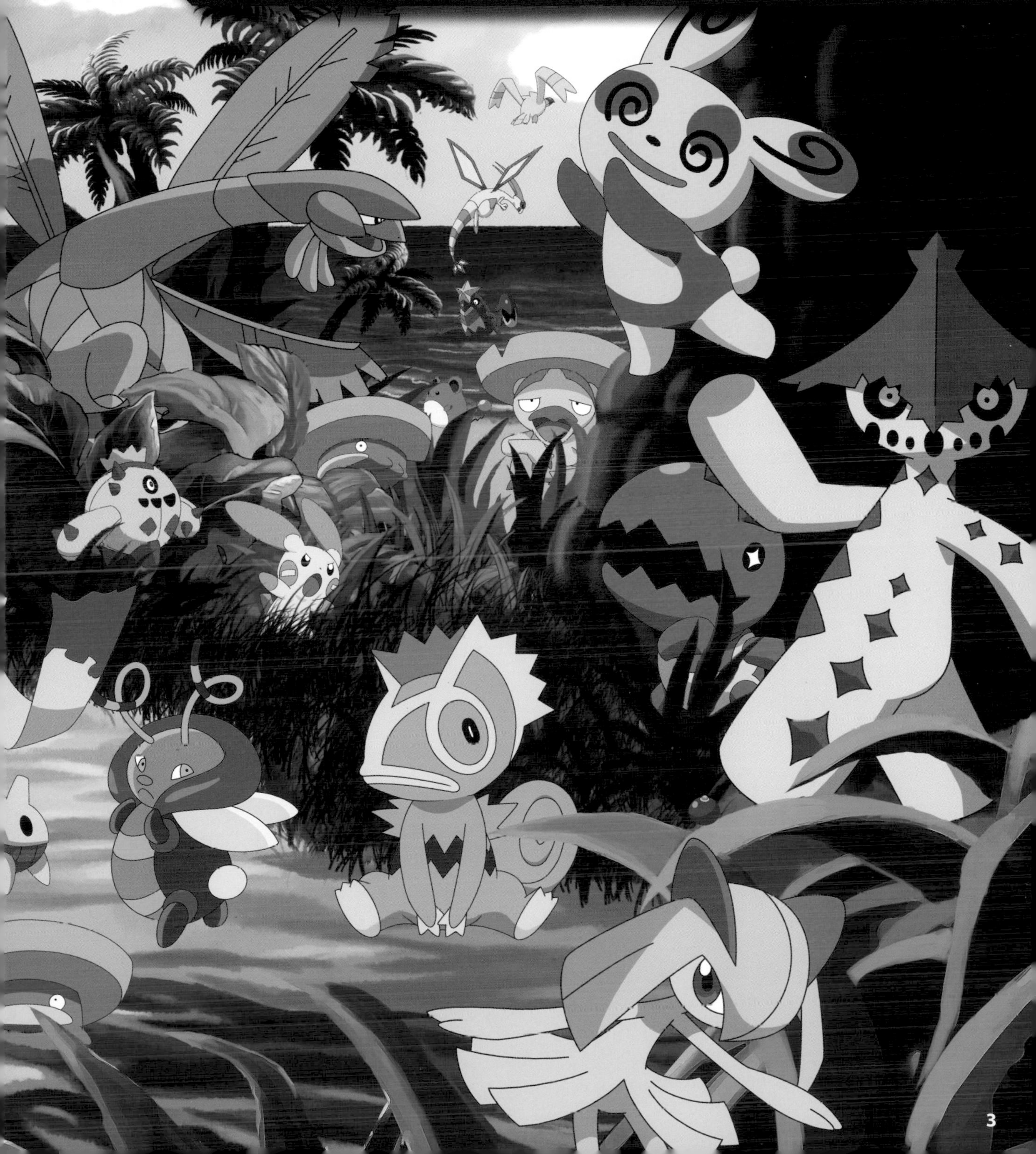

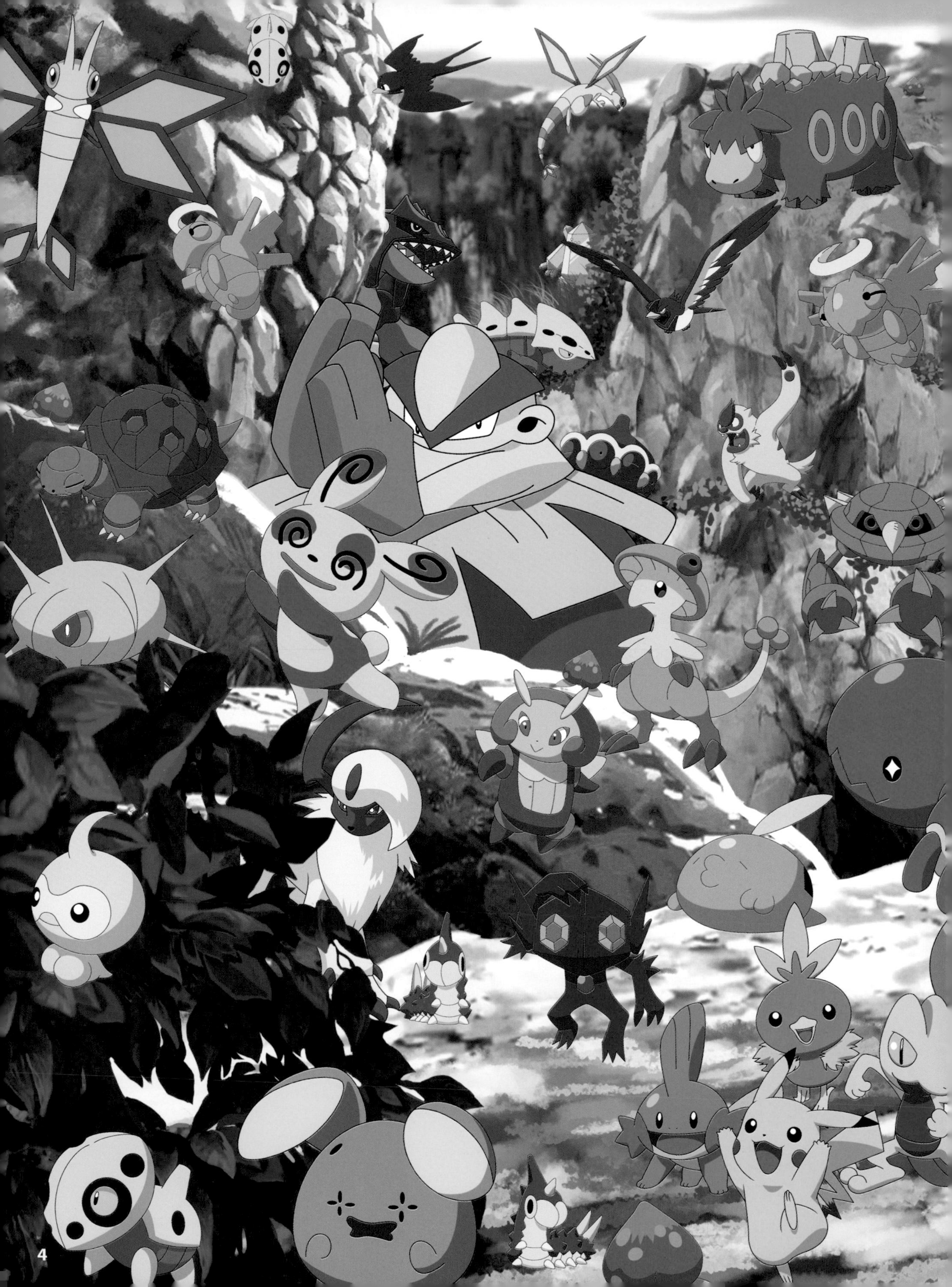

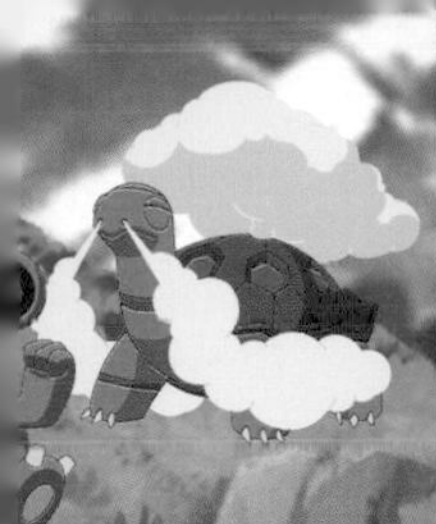

IN THE HEART OF THE MOUNTAINS

To reach the closest town, our friends have to travel through the mountains. Legend has it that the region was created by the Legendary Pokémon Kyogre and Groudon. Kyogre created the ocean, while Groudon created the continent!

LOOK FOR...

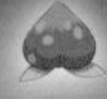

×6

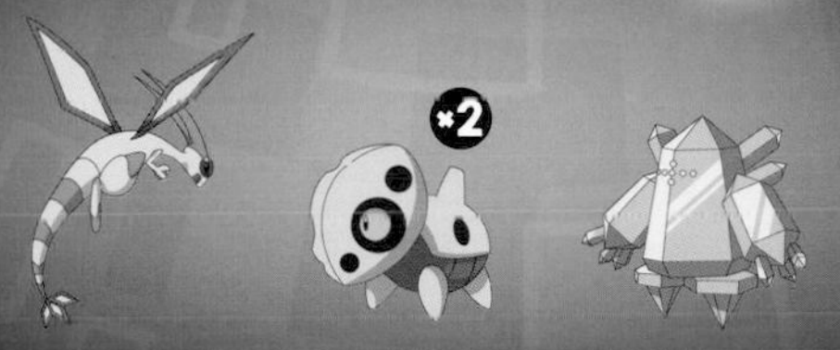

×2

Flygon Aron Regice

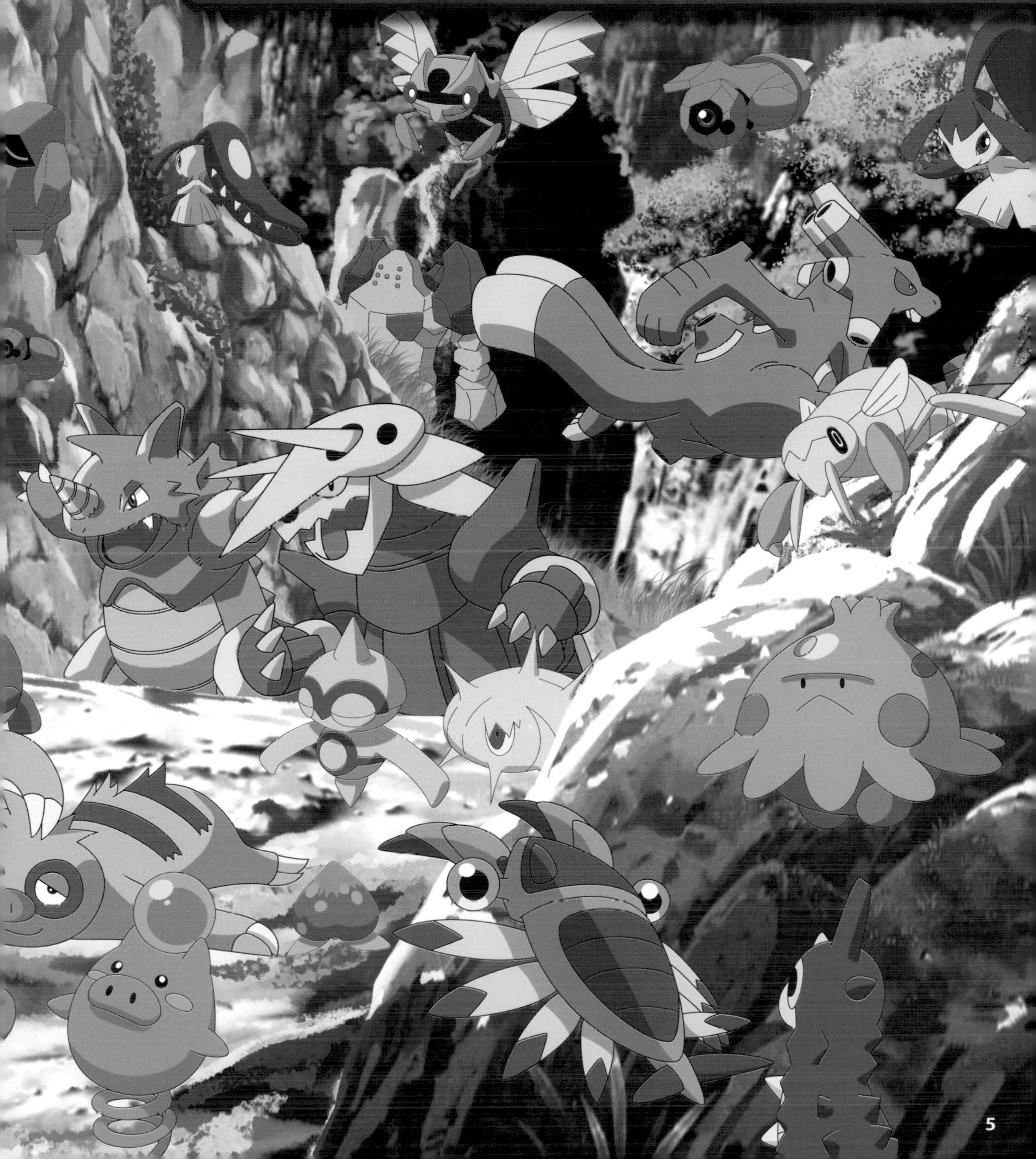

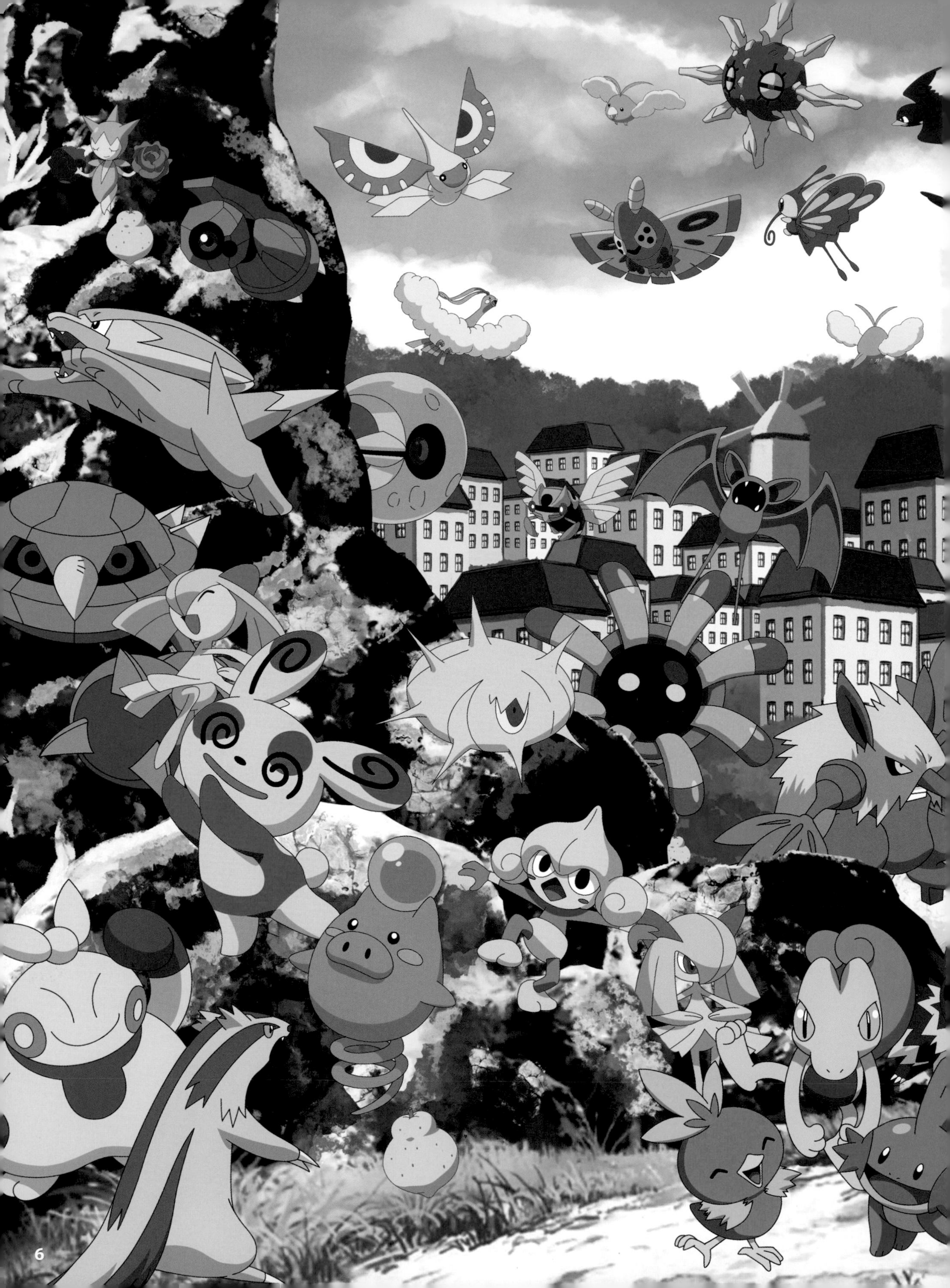

SILENCE, PLEASE!

Our friends finally catch sight of the town! Fortunately there's not far to go, but the impatient Pokémon start running in every direction! Hariyama can't hear anything. Everyone calm down!

LOOK FOR... ×4

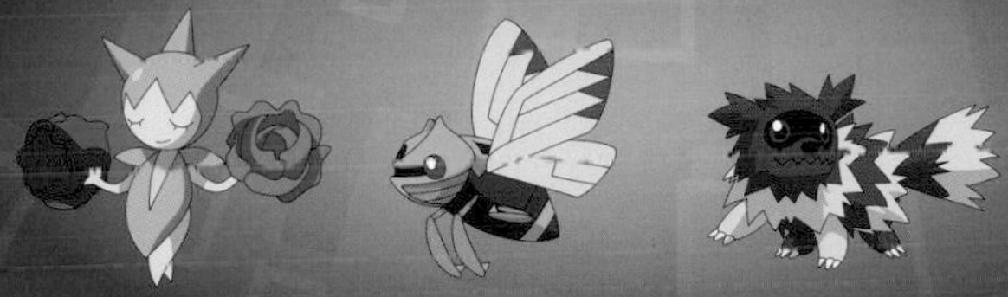

Roselia **Ninjask** **Zigzagoon**

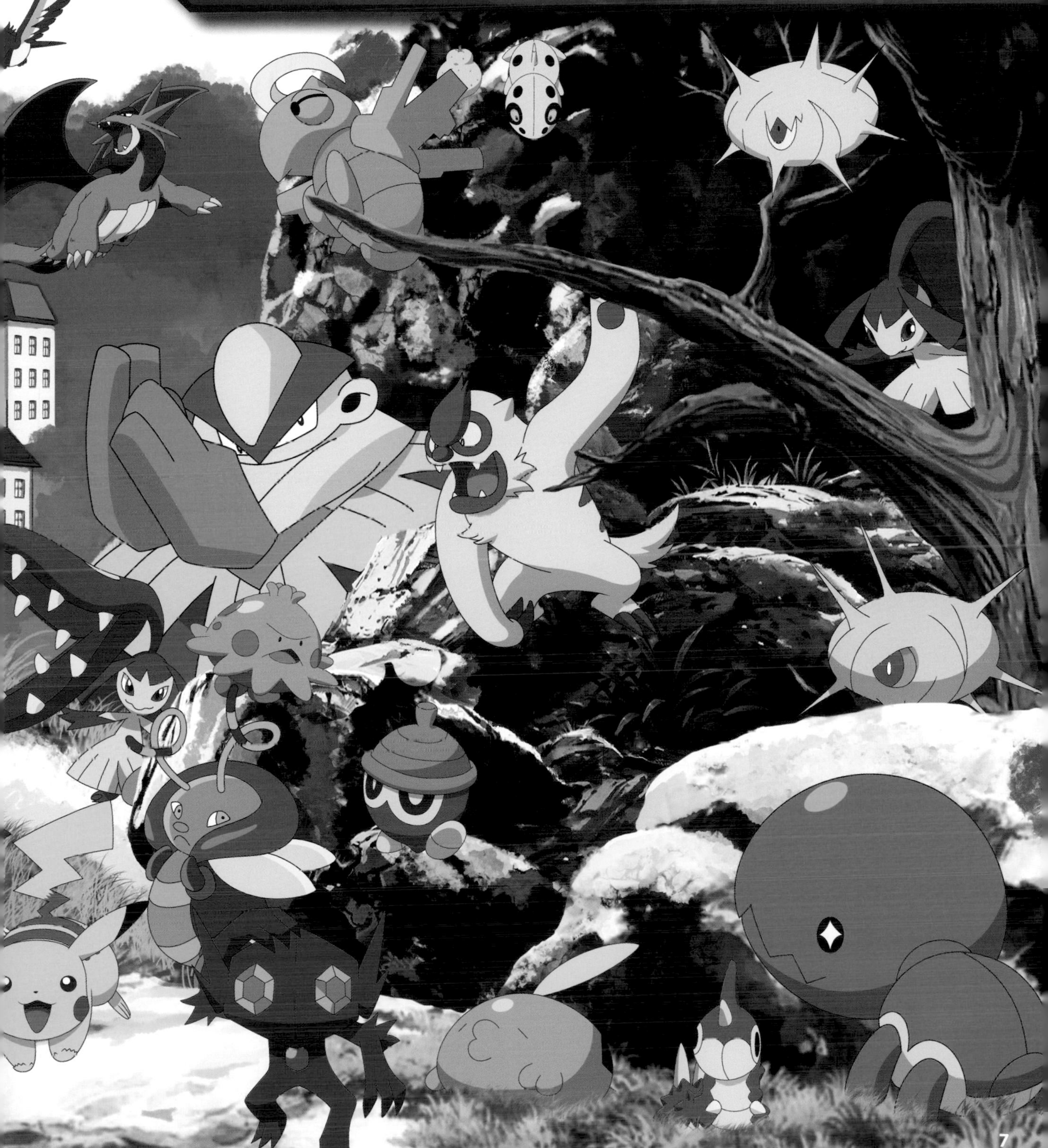

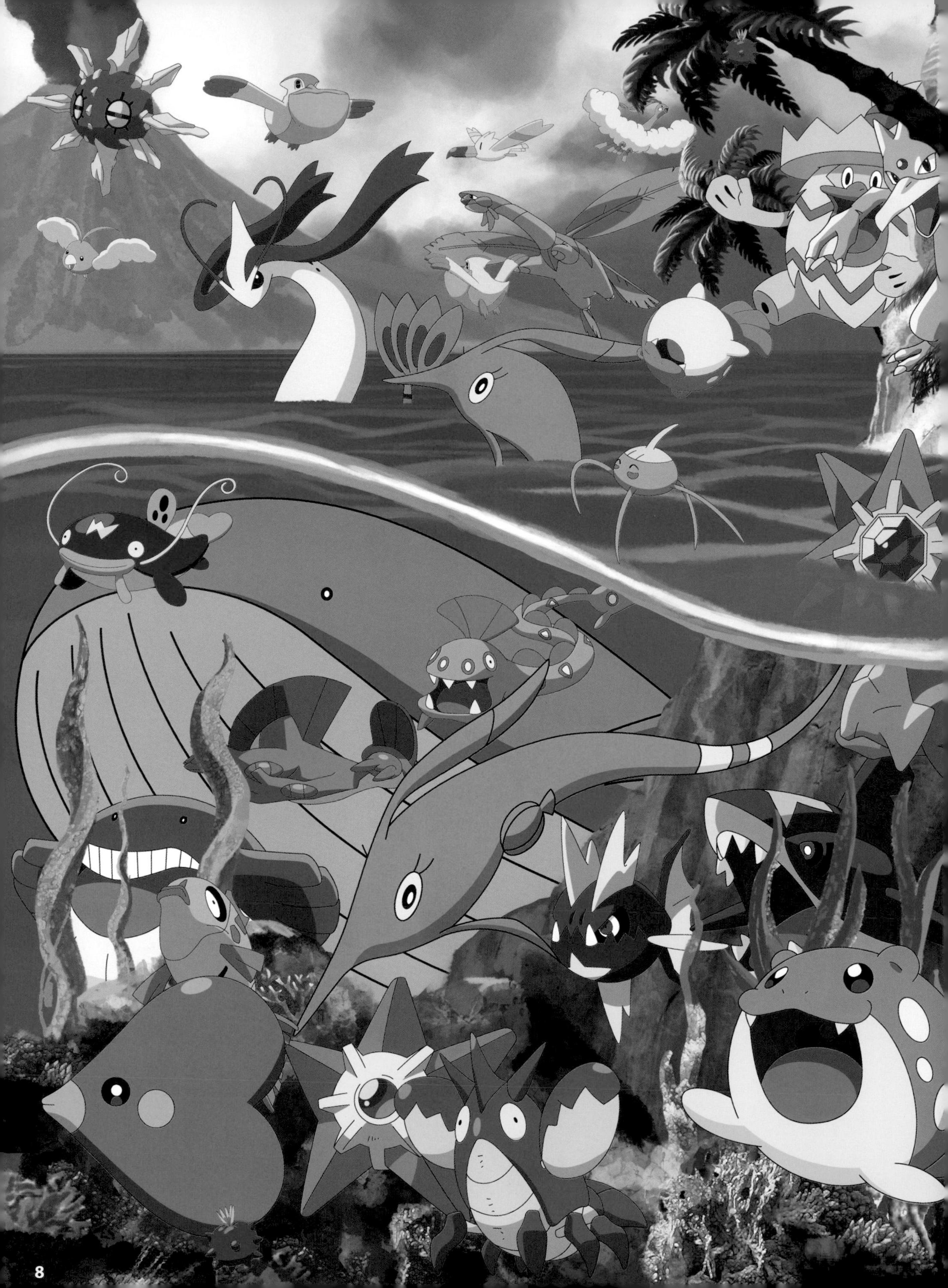

A REFRESHING BREAK

After their brief stop in town, our four friends decide to climb near a reef, where countless Water-type Pokémon are having fun. The sea is calm and it's a beautiful day. Let's join in!

LOOK FOR...

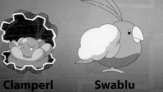

×5

Clamperl

Swablu

Spheal ×2

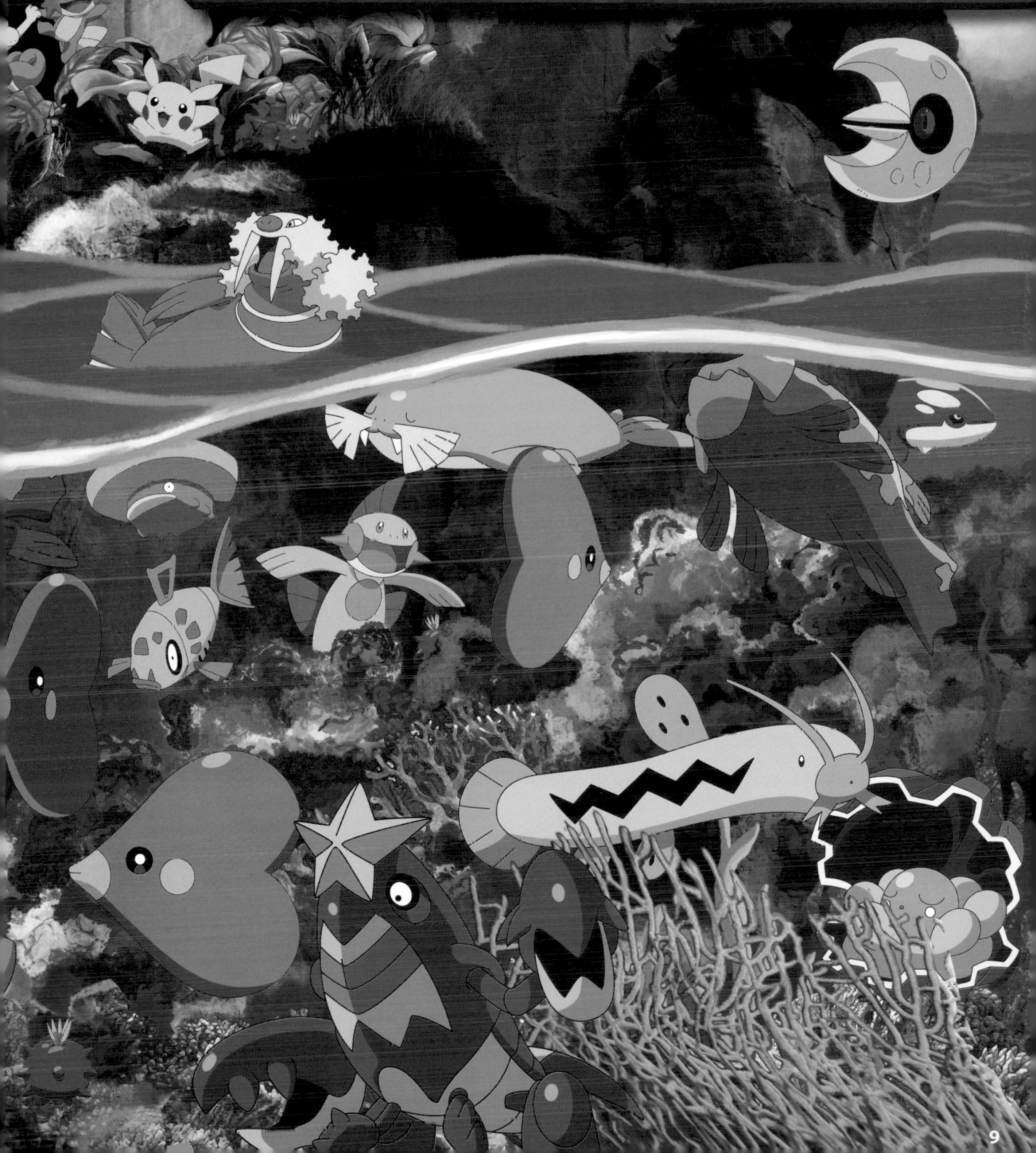

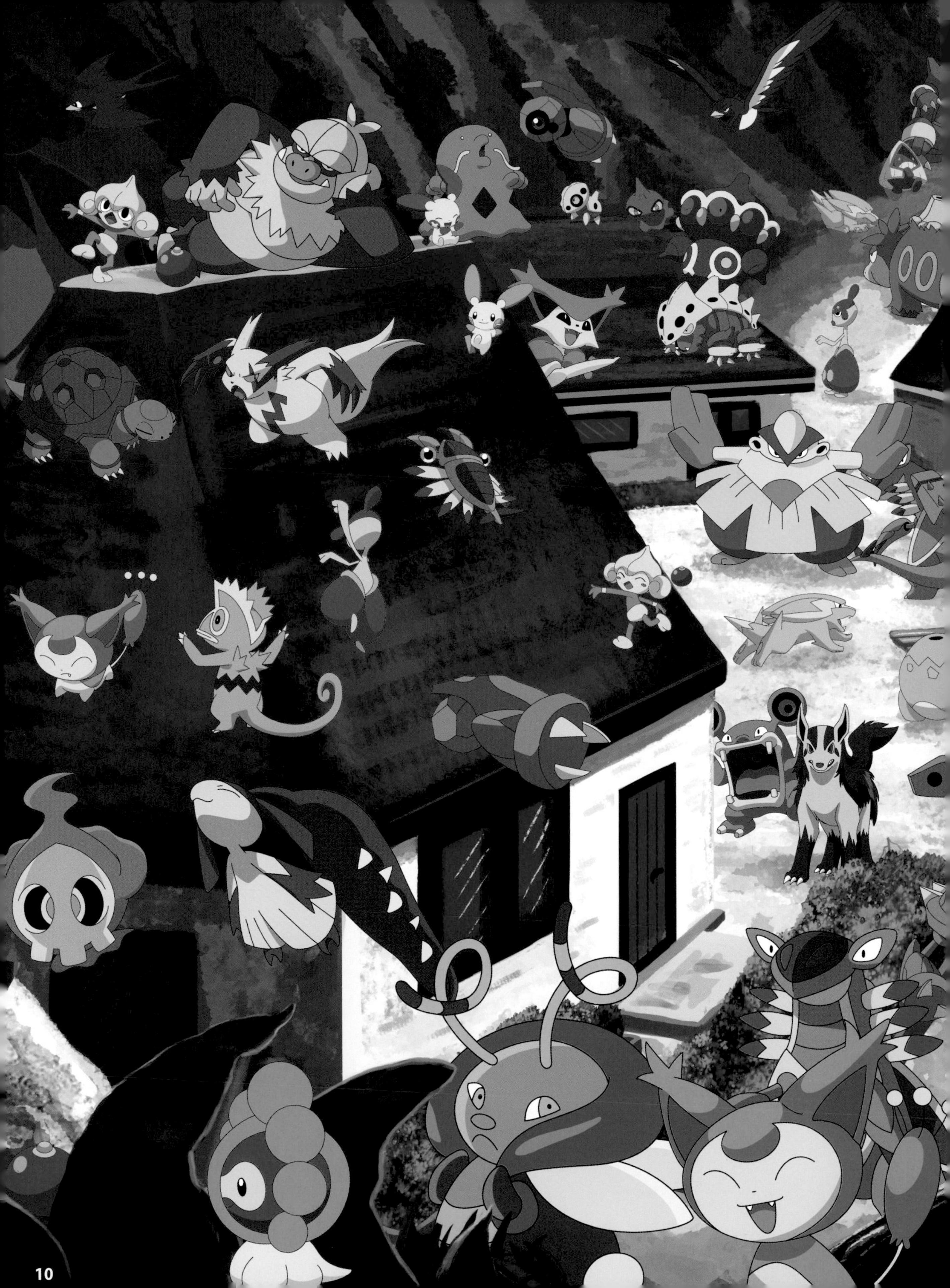

THE VILLAGE

Our friends deserve a little break after that aquatic escapade! Pikachu is taking a nap, but Mudkip, Treecko, and Torchic are still full of energy! Wake up, Pikachu! The adventure continues!

LOOK FOR...

×7

×3 **Meditite**

Loudred

Shuppet

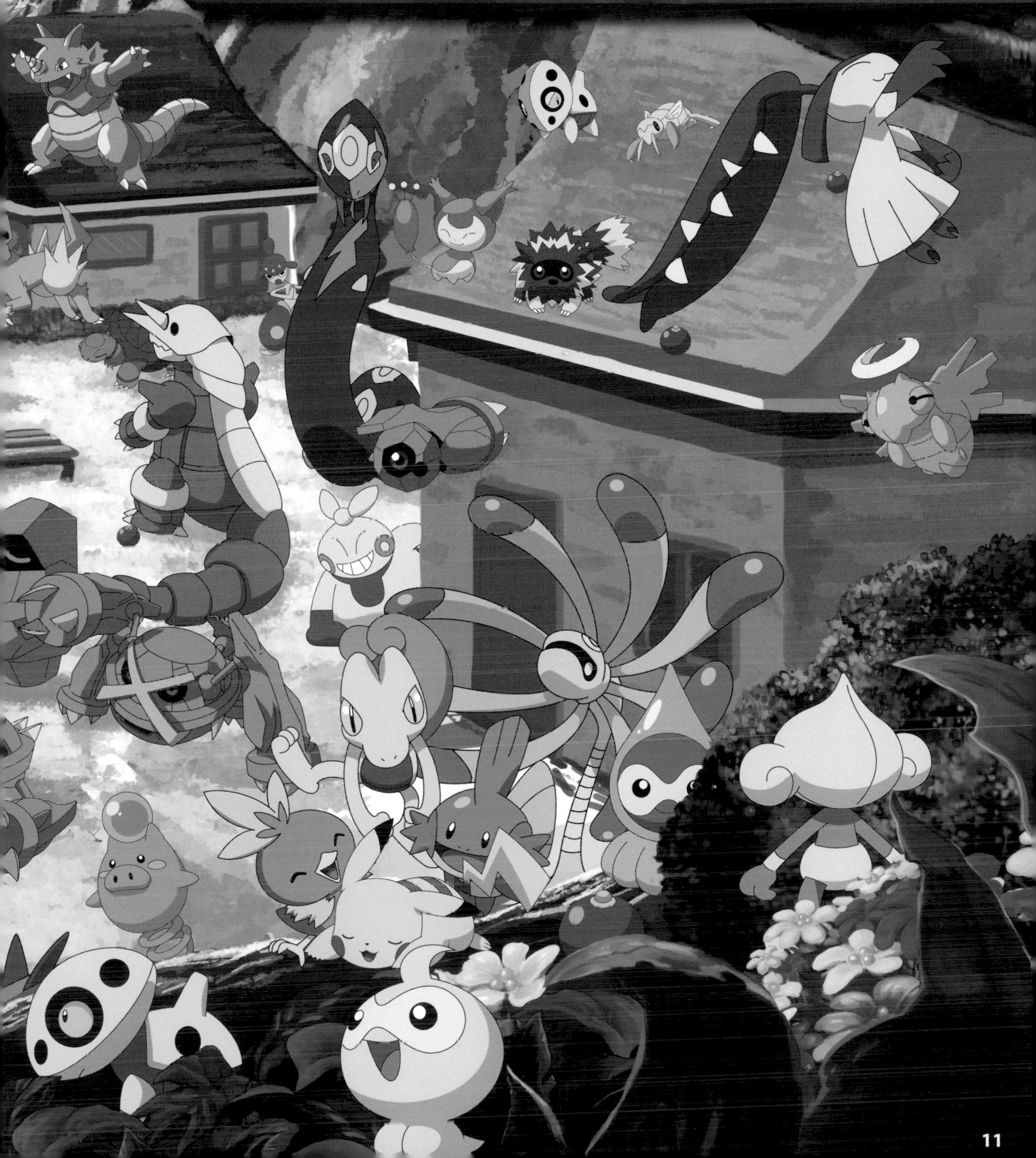

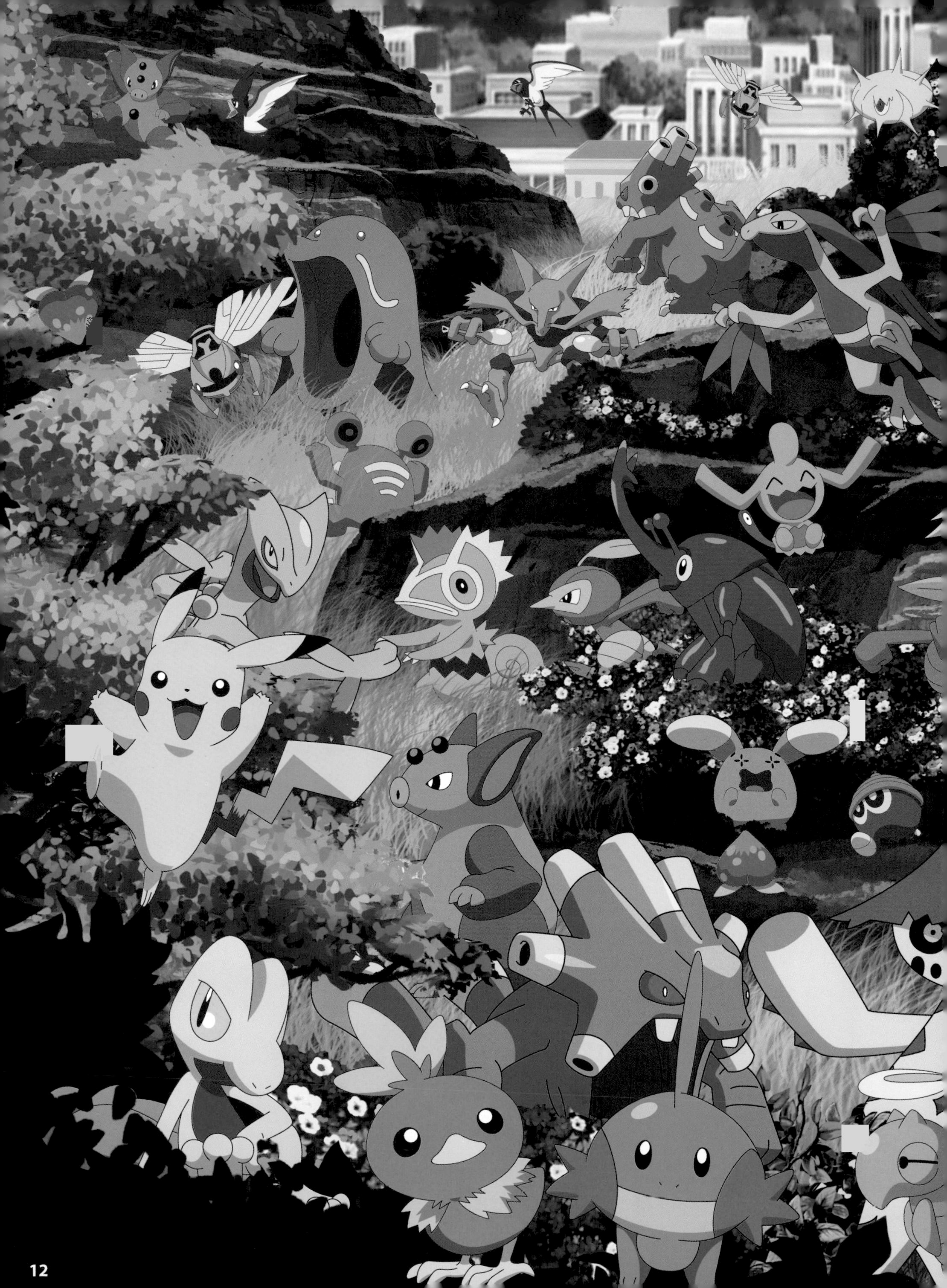

FLOWER HILL

Our friends are well rested and ready to get back on the road! There's still a long way to go, but Pikachu and all the Pokémon are as enthusiastic as ever!

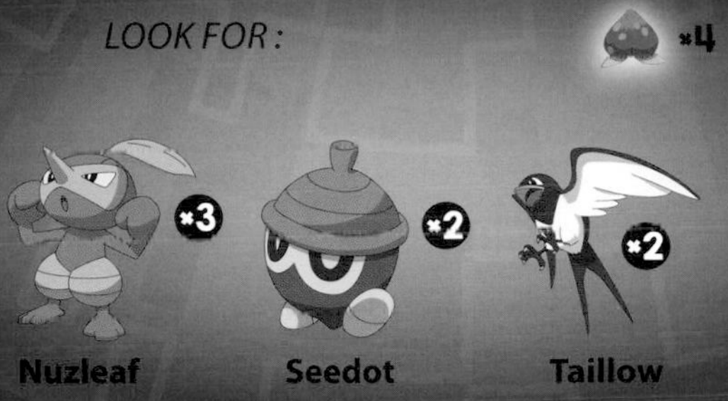
LOOK FOR :
×4
×3
Nuzleaf
×2
Seedot
×2
Taillow

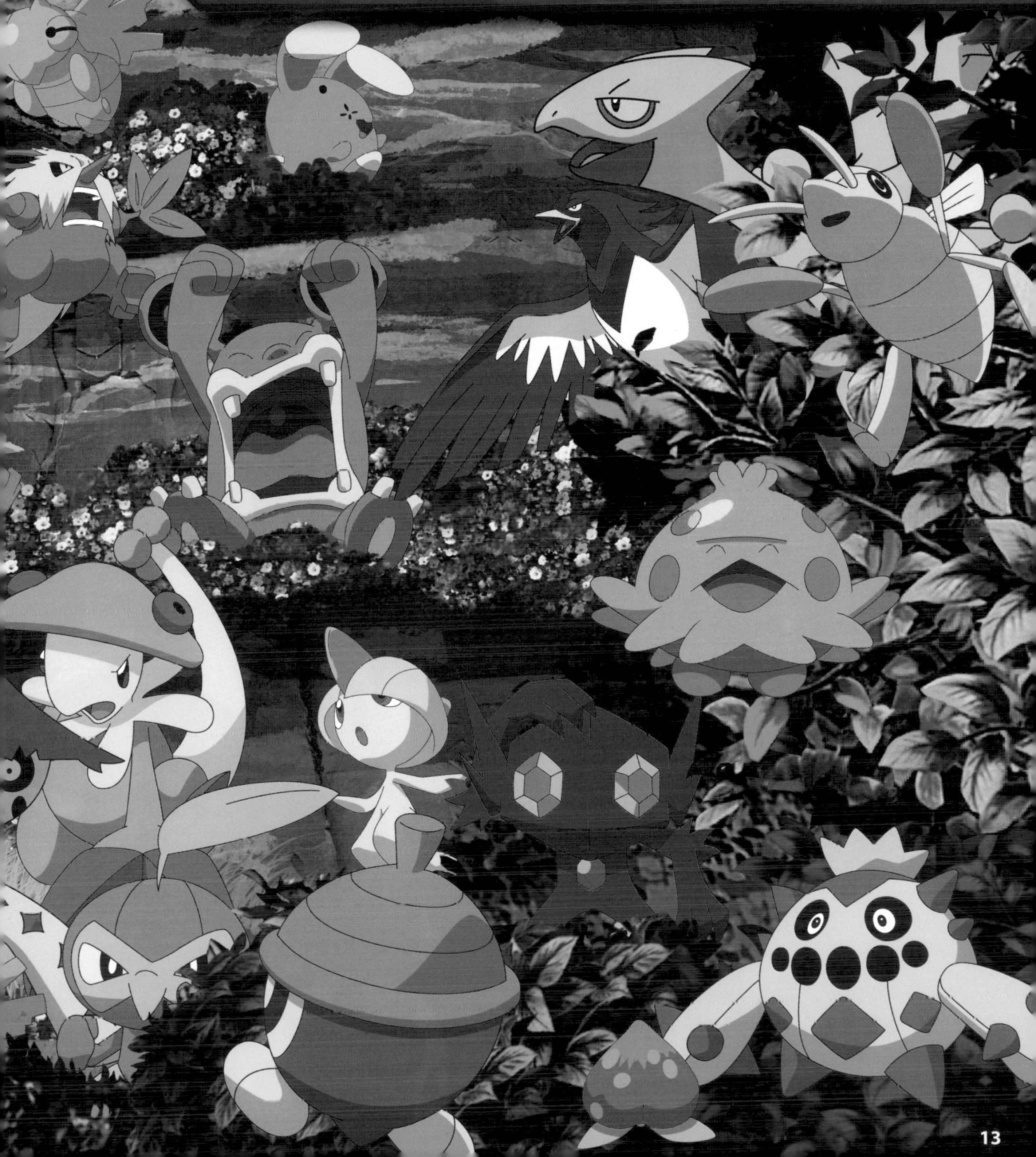

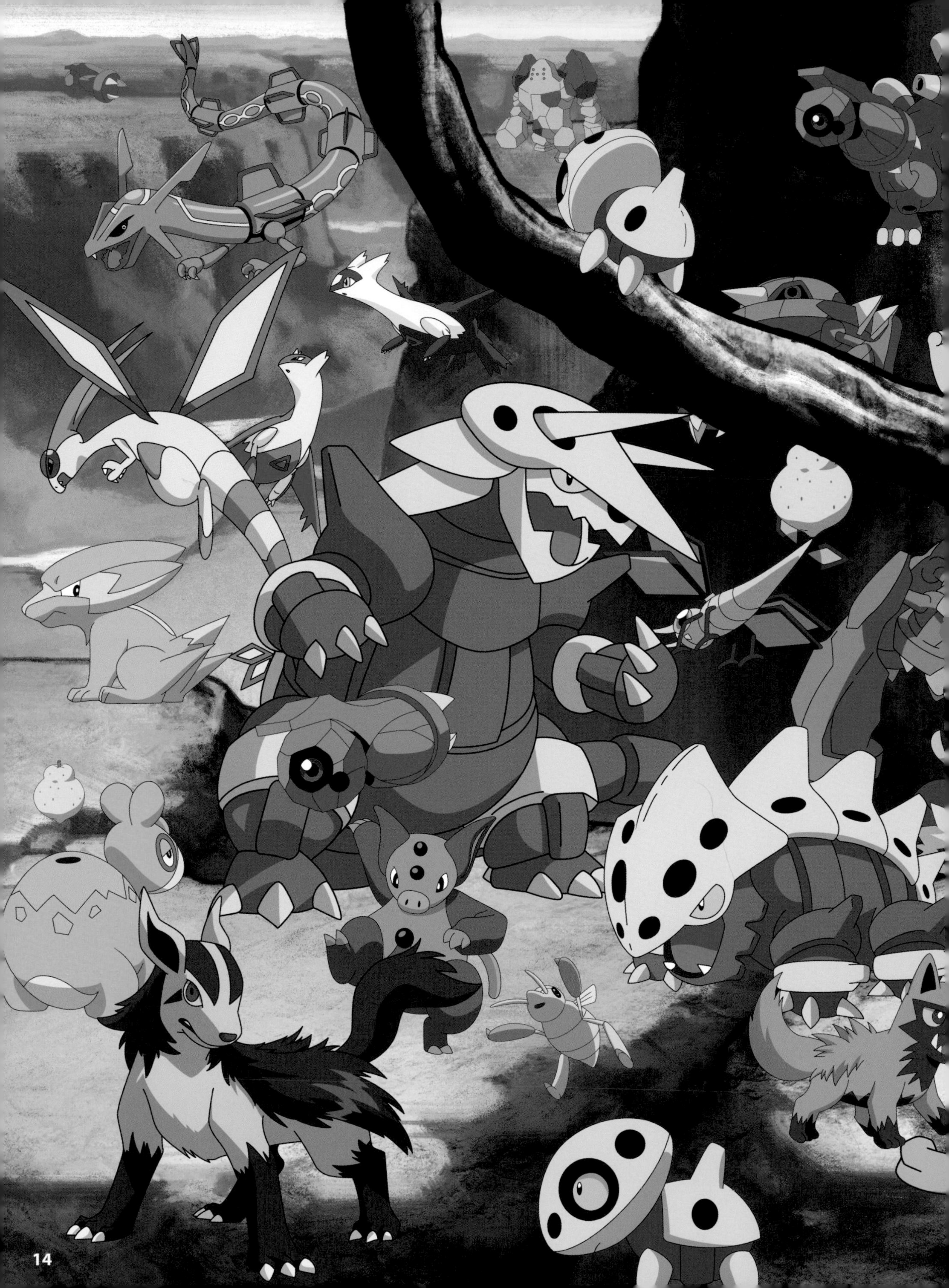

THE DESERT

Our friends continue their exploration of Hoenn and must now pass through the dry plains of the region. It's very hot, and the Pokémon are really thirsty... To make the trek interesting, Treecko, Torchic, and Mudkip have decided to start a race. Who will win?

LOOK FOR...

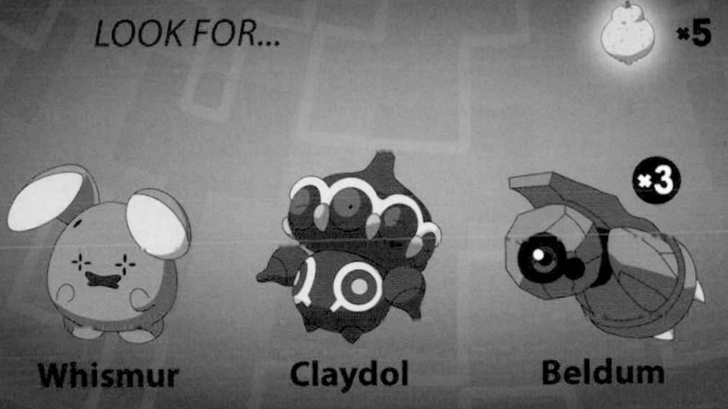

×5
×3
Whismur
Claydol
Beldum

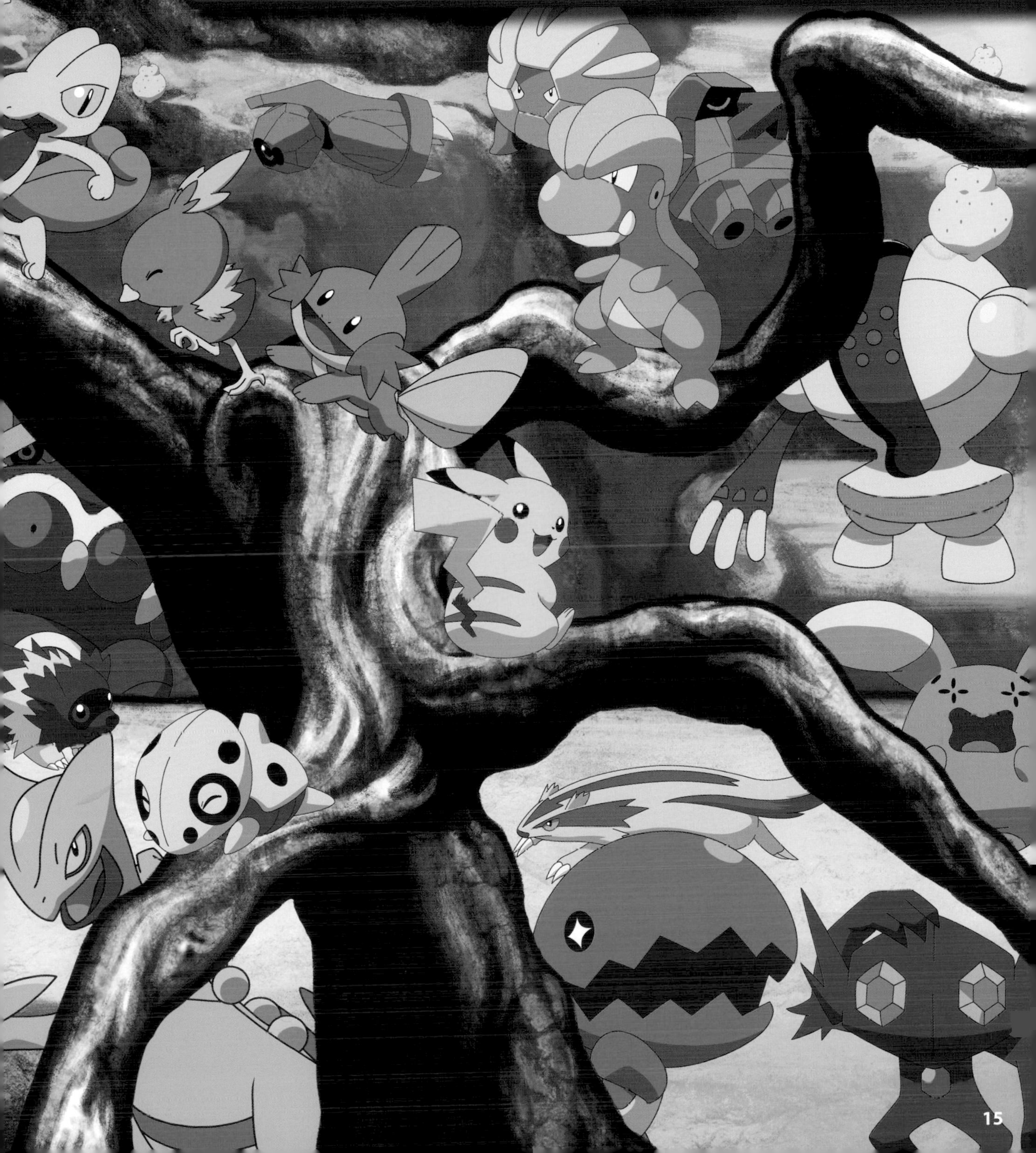

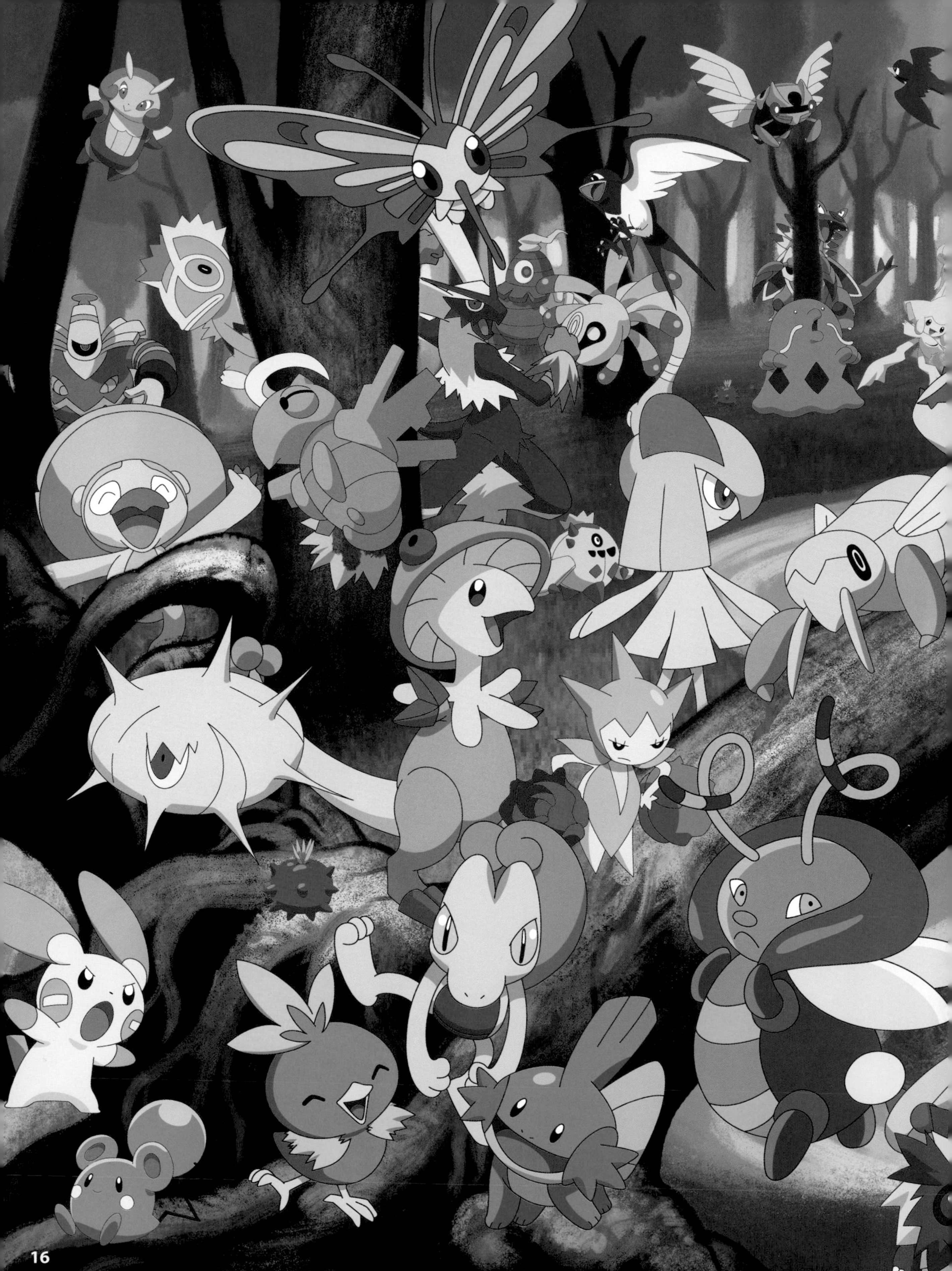

THE END OF THE ROAD

To get back to town and finish their journey, the Pokémon must go through a dense forest. It's a long way home, but a lot of Pokémon are there to make the hike more thrilling! Pikachu's playing hide-and-seek. Can you see where?

LOOK FOR...

×4

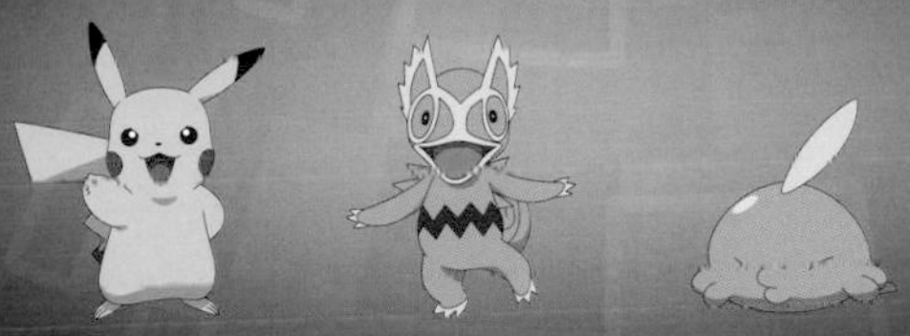

Pikachu

Kecleon

Gulpin

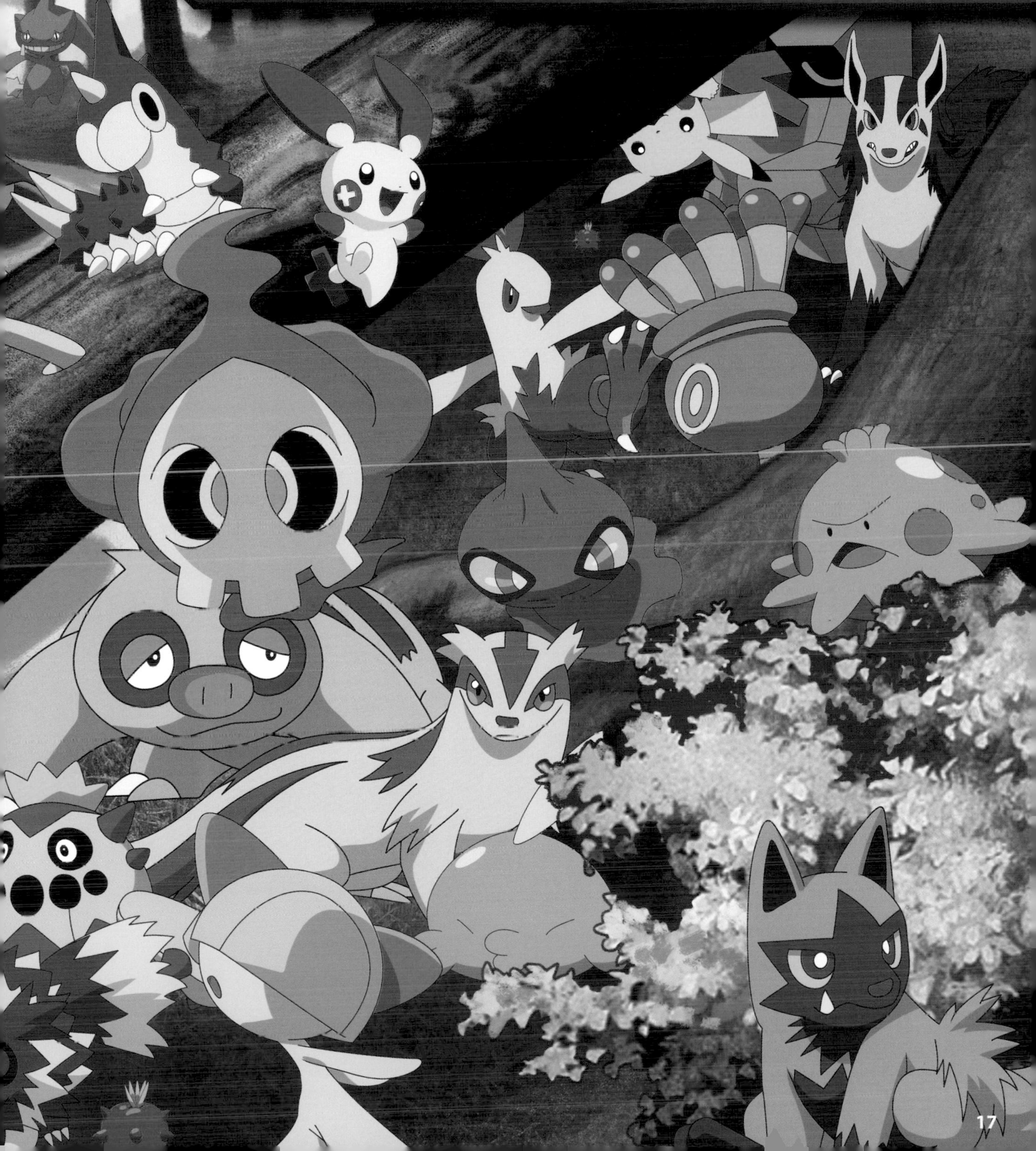

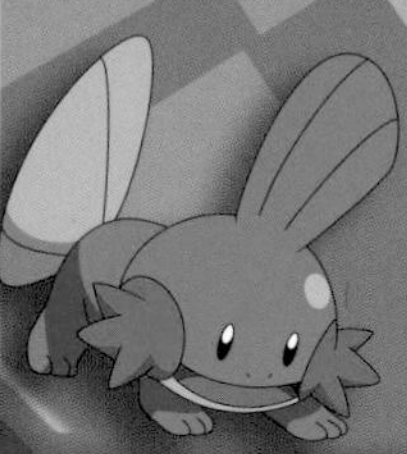

THE ULTIMATE CHALLENGE

Have you completed your mission and found all of the Pokémon in each of the scenes? If so, you're ready for the next challenge! Only the most exceptional Pokémon Trainers will succeed!

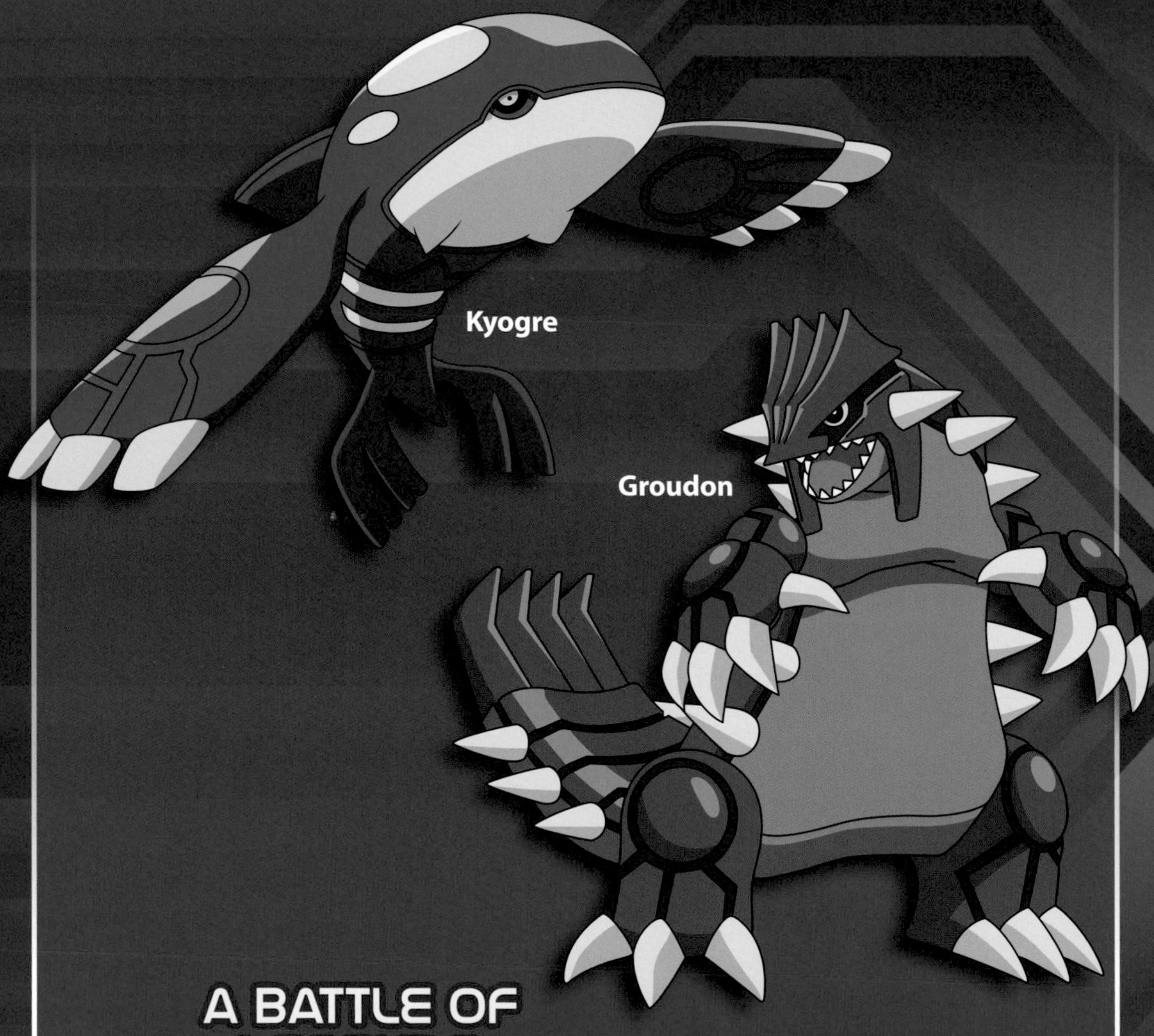
Kyogre
Groudon

A BATTLE OF LEGENDS

Kyogre and Groudon are hidden in the scenes of this story.

YOU MUST FIND THEM!

GUIDE TO THE POKÉMON OF HOENN

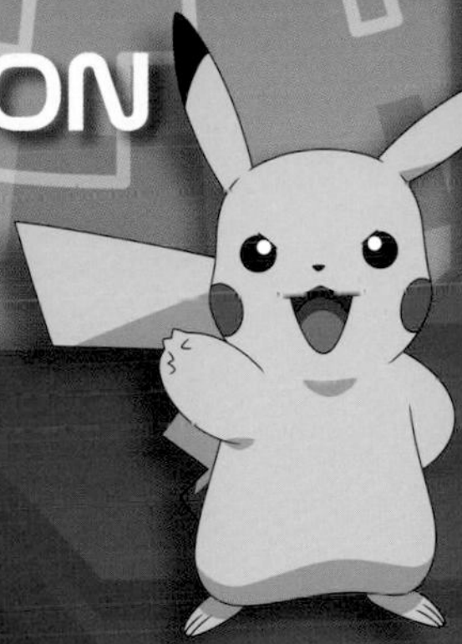

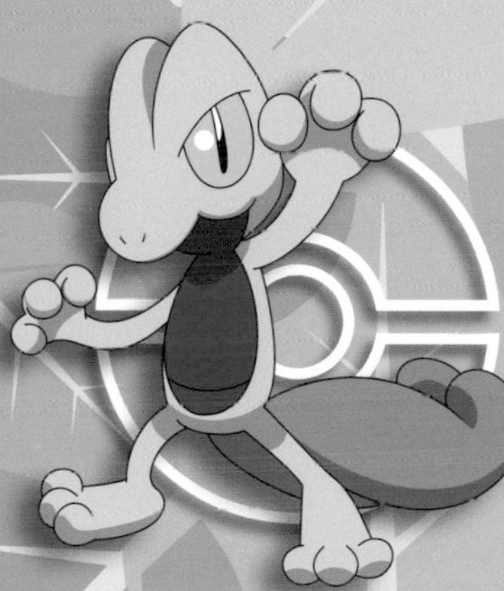

CATEGORY:
WOOD GECKO POKÉMON
TYPE: GRASS
HEIGHT: 1'08"
WEIGHT: 11.0 lbs
EVOLUTION:
Treecko ➛ Grovyle ➛ Sceptile ➛ Mega Sceptile

TREECKO

Treecko can climb up steep walls thanks to the tiny spikes on the bottom of its feet. Its tail can detect meteorological shifts.

AZURILL

When faced with tough opponents, Azurill fights by whipping them with its tail, which is larger than its own body.

CATEGORY:
POLKA DOT POKÉMON
TYPE: NORMAL-FAIRY
HEIGHT: 0'08"
WEIGHT: 4.4 lbs
EVOLUTION:
Azurill ➛ Marill ➛ Azumarill

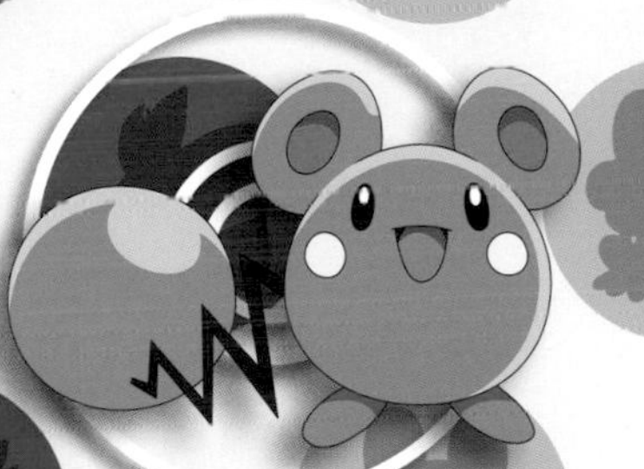

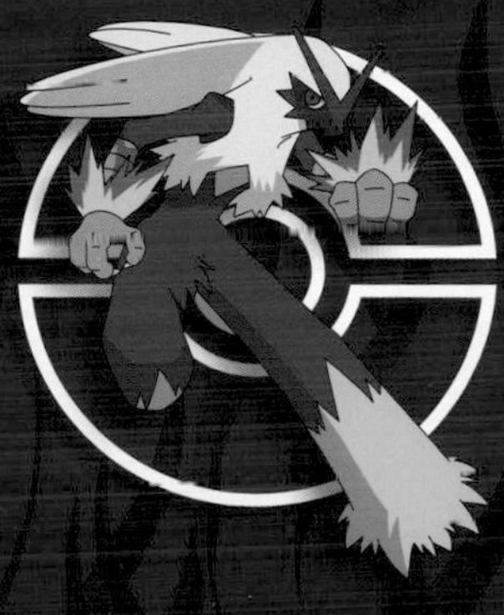

CATEGORY:
BLAZE POKÉMON
TYPE: FIRE FIGHTING
HEIGHT: 6'03"
WEIGHT: 114.6 lbs
EVOLUTION:
Torchic ➛ Combusken ➛ **Blaziken** ➛ Mega Blaziken

BLAZIKEN

Blaziken can create fire from its wrists to make its punches flaming hot. Its legs are so powerful it can jump from building to building.

CATEGORY:
LOUD NOISE POKÉMON
TYPE: NORMAL
HEIGHT: 4'11"
WEIGHT: 185.2 lbs
EVOLUTION:
Whismur → Loudred → **Exploud**

EXPLOUD

All the tubes on Exploud's body produce different sounds when air passes through them. Its battle cry shakes the ground around it and can be heard from over a mile away.

WHISMUR

Enemies who attack Whismur scatter at the sound of its cry, which is as loud as a jet engine. It goes silent once its ears close up again.

CATEGORY:
WHISPER POKÉMON
TYPE: NORMAL
HEIGHT: 2'00"
WEIGHT: 35.9 lbs
EVOLUTION:
Whismur → Loudred → Exploud

CATEGORY:
MUD FISH POKÉMON
TYPE: WATER-GROUND
HEIGHT: 2'04"
WEIGHT: 61.7 lbs
EVOLUTION:
Mudkip → **Marshtomp**
→ Swampert → Mega Swampert

MARSHTOMP

Thanks to its sturdy legs, Marshtomp can walk without any difficulty on steep or boggy terrain.

COMBUSKEN

Combusken's extremely fast kicks and piercing battle cry make it a formidable opponent. Its flames double in intensity when it's fighting.

CATEGORY:
YOUNG FOWL POKÉMON
TYPE: FIRE-FIGHTING
HEIGHT: 2'11"
WEIGHT: 43.0 lbs
EVOLUTION:
Torchic → **Combusken** →
Blaziken → Mega Blaziken

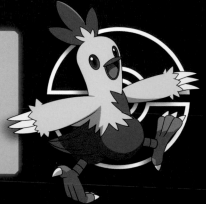

MUDKIP

The fin on Mudkip's head allows it to analyze currents. It's strong enough to lift rocks, and its tail fin gives it an excellent speed advantage when swimming.

CATEGORY:
MUD FISH POKÉMON
TYPE: WATER
HEIGHT: 1'04"
WEIGHT: 16.8 lbs
EVOLUTION:
Mudkip ➛ Marshtomp ➛ Swampert ➛ Mega Swampert

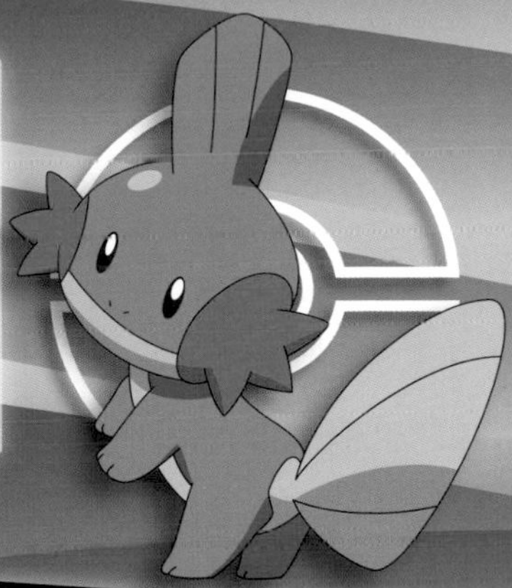

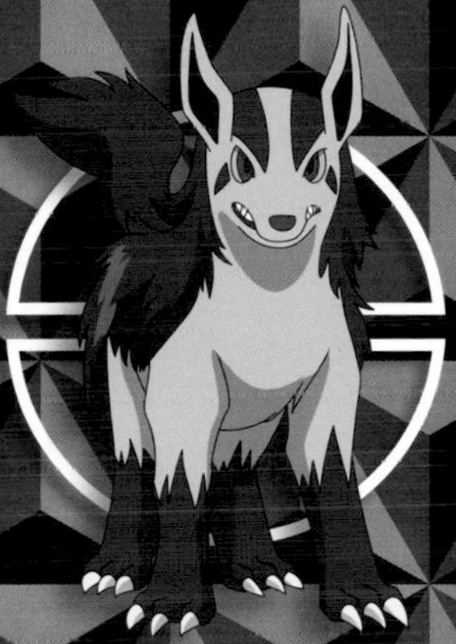

CATEGORY:
BITE POKÉMON
TYPE: DARK
HEIGHT: 3'03"
WEIGHT: 81.6 lbs
EVOLUTION:
Poochyena ➛ **Mightyena**

MIGHTYENA

When in the wild, Mightyena will go on a chase in silence and defeat their opponents as a pack. Trainers believe these instincts make Mightyena a great partner.

GROUDON

Legend has it that the heat generated by Groudon's body is what caused the oceans to dry and the continents to form. This Pokémon falls into a deep slumber after combat with Kyogre.

CATEGORY:
CONTINENT POKÉMON
TYPE: GROUND
HEIGHT: 11'06"
WEIGHT: 2094.4 lbs
EVOLUTION:
Groudon ➛ Primal Groudon

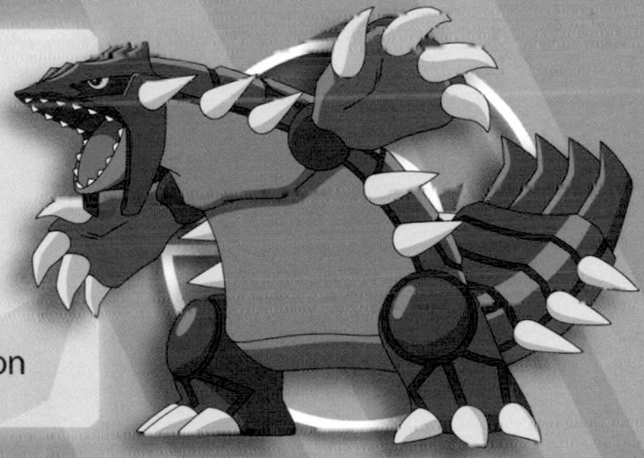

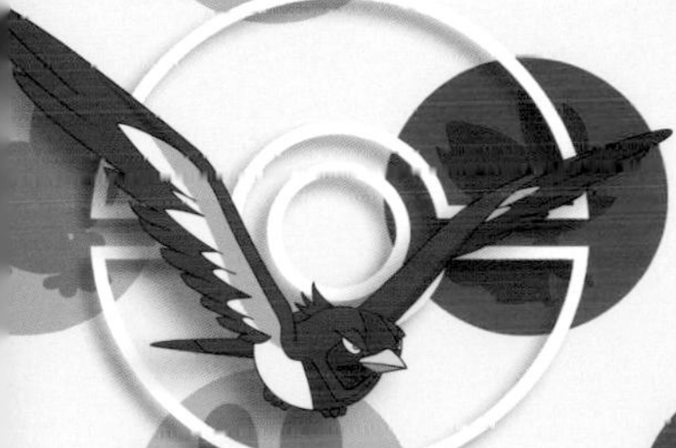

CATEGORY:
SWALLOW POKÉMON
TYPE: NORMAL-FLYING
HEIGHT: 2'04"
WEIGHT: 43.7 lbs
EVOLUTION:
Taillow ➛ **Swellow**

SWELLOW

Rising gracefully into the sky, Swellow will dive-bomb to catch its prey on the ground. Its long tail feathers stand completely straight when it's in good health.

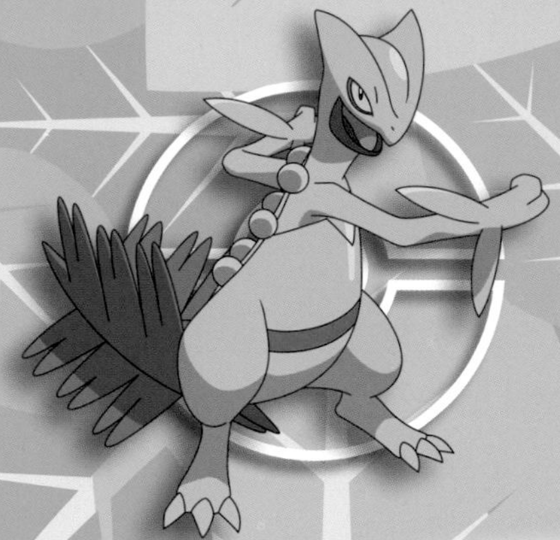

SCEPTILE

Sceptile has an advantage in the jungle, where it reaches great heights when it leaps and attacks by slashing with the sharp leaves on its arms.

CATEGORY:
FOREST POKÉMON
TYPE: GRASS
HEIGHT: 5'07"
WEIGHT: 115.1 lbs
EVOLUTION:
Treecko ➛ Grovyle ➛ **Sceptile** ➛ Mega Sceptile

KECLEON

Kecleon is a master of the art of camouflage. It can change its body color to blend into its environment. However, the zigzag pattern can't shift.

CATEGORY:
COLOR SWAP POKÉMON
TYPE: NORMAL
HEIGHT: 3'03"
WEIGHT: 48.5 lbs
EVOLUTION:
This Pokémon does not evolve.

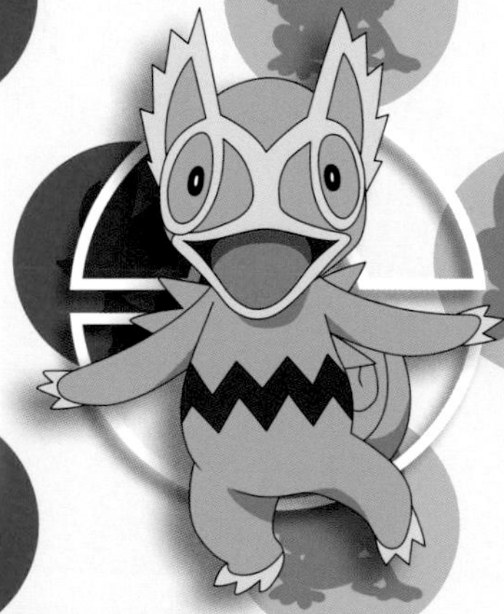

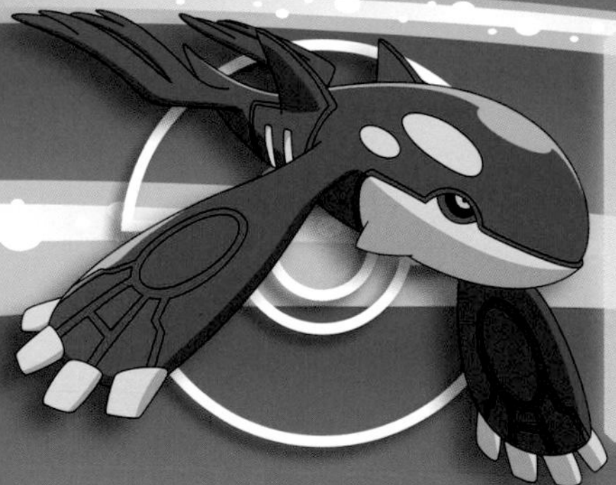

KYOGRE

It is said that Kyogre, the Pokémon that controls water, made the oceans larger by blanketing the land with heavy downpours and massive wave surges.

CATEGORY:
SEA BASIN POKÉMON
TYPE: WATER
HEIGHT: 14'09"
WEIGHT: 776.0 lbs
EVOLUTION:
Kyogre ➛ Primal Kyogre

SWAMPERT

Swampert is strong enough to tow ships while swimming. It hits its enemies with its enormous arms and can pulverize rocks to dust.

CATEGORY:
MUD FISH POKÉMON
TYPE: WATER-GROUND
HEIGHT: 4'11"
WEIGHT: 180.6 lbs
EVOLUTION:
Mudkip ➛ Marshtomp ➛ **Swampert** ➛ Mega Swampert

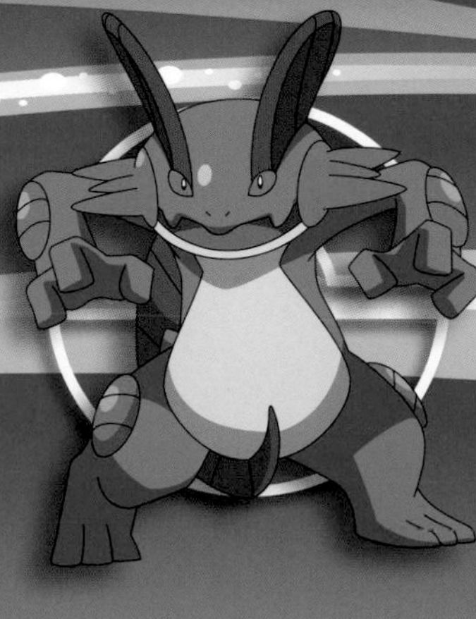

LATIAS

Latias can read the hearts of humans, and because of its high intelligence, it can also understand human speech. The specialized feathers that cover its body refract light.

CATEGORY:
EON POKÉMON
TYPE: DRAGON-PSYCHIC
HEIGHT: 4'07"
WEIGHT: 88.2 lbs
EVOLUTION:
Latias ➛ Mega Latias

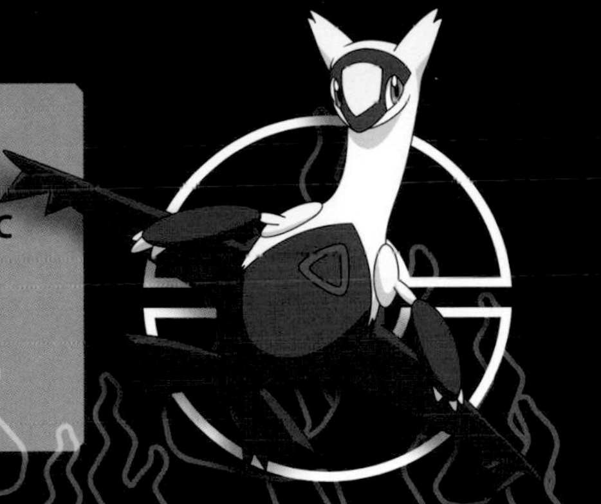

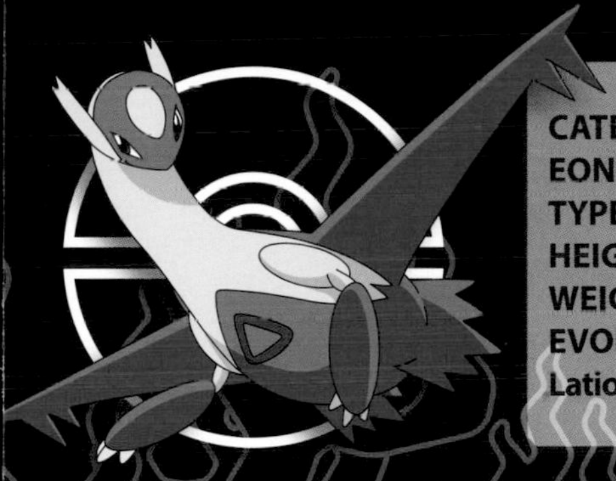

CATEGORY:
EON POKÉMON
TYPE: DRAGON-PSYCHIC
HEIGHT: 6'07"
WEIGHT: 132.3 lbs
EVOLUTION:
Latios ➛ Mega Latios

LATIOS

Latios becomes attached only to those with kind hearts. One Latios can transmit to another an image of what it sees or what it is thinking. It can fly faster than a jet plane.

LOMBRE

When Lombre suspects someone is fishing on the sunny shore where it lives, it likes to mess around and stir the water.

CATEGORY:
JOLLY POKÉMON
TYPE: WATER-GRASS
HEIGHT: 3'11"
WEIGHT: 71.6 lbs
EVOLUTION:
Lotad ➛ **Lombre** ➛ Ludicolo

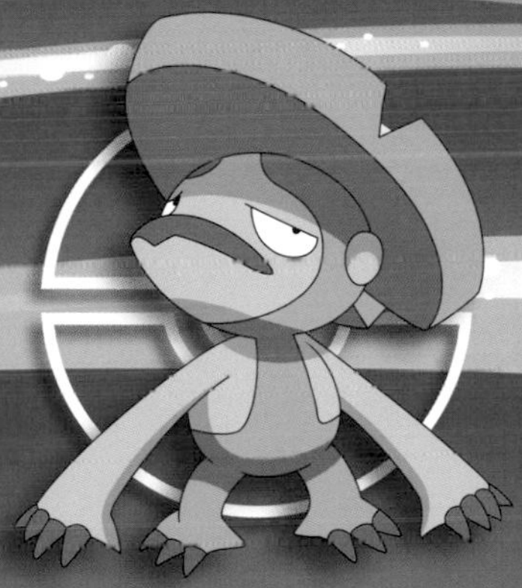

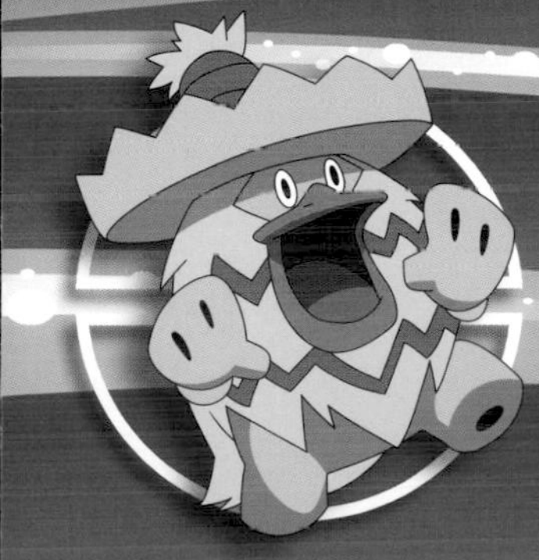

CATEGORY:
CAREFREE POKÉMON
TYPE: WATER-GRASS
HEIGHT: 4'11"
WEIGHT: 121.3 lbs
EVOLUTION:
Lotad ➛ Lombre ➛ **Ludicolo**

LUDICOLO

Ludicolo can't help but dance when it hears good music. Rhythmic music gives it energy!

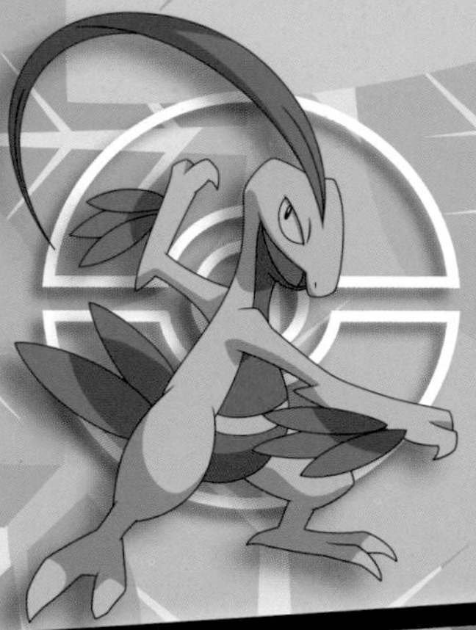

GROVYLE

Nimble and agile, Grovyle is an excellent jumper. It lives in the dense jungle, where it jumps from branch to branch.

CATEGORY:
WOOD GECKO POKÉMON
TYPE: GRASS
HEIGHT: 2'11"
WEIGHT: 47.6 lbs
EVOLUTION:
Treecko ➛ **Grovyle** ➛ Sceptile ➛ Mega Sceptile

POOCHYENA

Poochyena is second to none when it comes to tracking. It uses its sense of smell to follow any trace of its adversaries, even those who disappeared long ago.

CATEGORY:
BITE POKÉMON
TYPE: DARK
HEIGHT: 1'08"
WEIGHT: 30.0 lbs
EVOLUTION:
Poochyena ➛ Mightyena

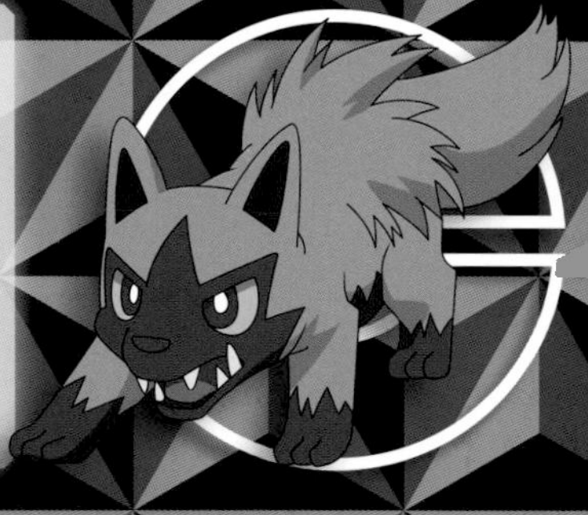

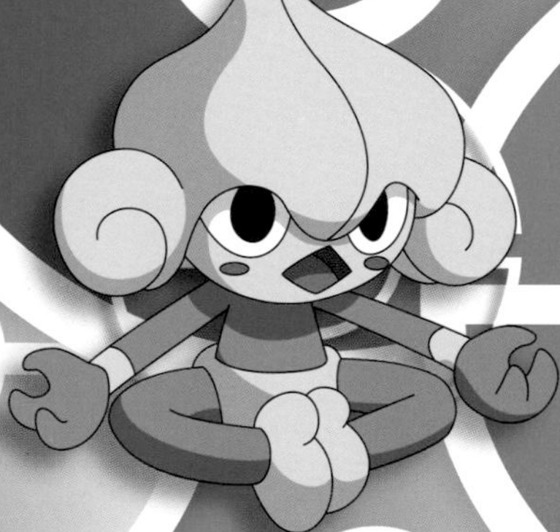

MEDITITE

It trains every day, increasing the strength of its willpower through meditation. However, because Meditite has a short attention span, it never finishes its training.

CATEGORY:
MEDITATE POKÉMON
TYPE: FIGHTING-PSYCHIC
HEIGHT: 2'00"
WEIGHT: 24.7 lbs
EVOLUTION:
Meditite ➛ Medicham ➛ Mega Medicham

SHEDINJA

It is said Shedinja steals the souls of those who look into its shell. In certain circumstances, this Pokémon appears in Ninjask's stead when Nincada evolves.

CATEGORY:
SHED POKÉMON
TYPE: BUG-GHOST
HEIGHT: 2'07"
WEIGHT: 2.6 lbs
EVOLUTION:
Nincada ➛ Ninjask or **Shedinja**

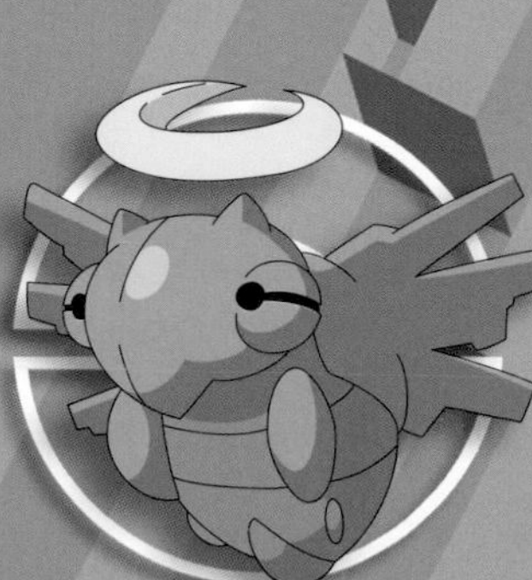

MAWILE

The large jaws attached to Mawile's head are so strong they can grind a steel rod.

CATEGORY:
DECEIVER POKÉMON
TYPE: STEEL-FAIRY
HEIGHT: 2'00"
WEIGHT: 25.4 lbs
EVOLUTION:
Mawile ➛ Mega Mawile

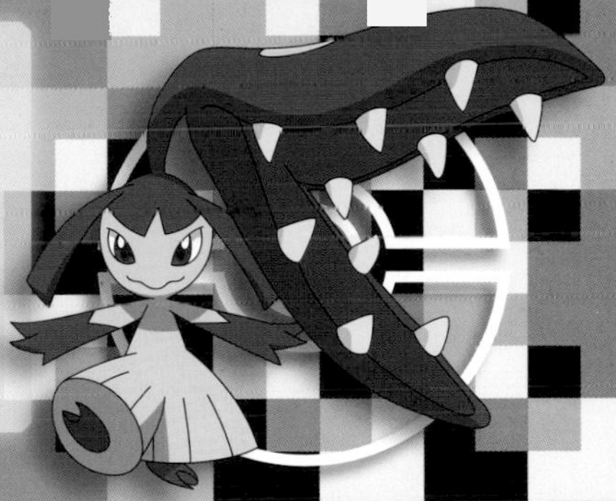

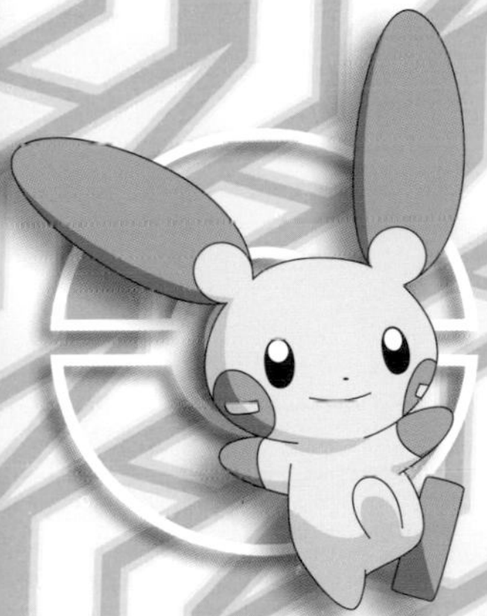

CATEGORY:
CHEERING POKÉMON
TYPE: ELECTRIC
HEIGHT: 1'04"
WEIGHT: 9.3 lbs
EVOLUTION:
This Pokémon does not evolve.

MINUN

Minun emits sparks to motivate its friends. The electricity generated by this Pokémon helps people relax. It's also good for their health.

NINCADA

Nincada doesn't have very well-developed vision because it lives underground. It uses its antennae to sense its surroundings while it eats roots and branches.

CATEGORY:
TRAINEE POKÉMON
TYPE: BUG-GROUND
HEIGHT: 1'08"
WEIGHT: 12.1 lbs
EVOLUTION:
Nincada ➛ Ninjask or Shedinja

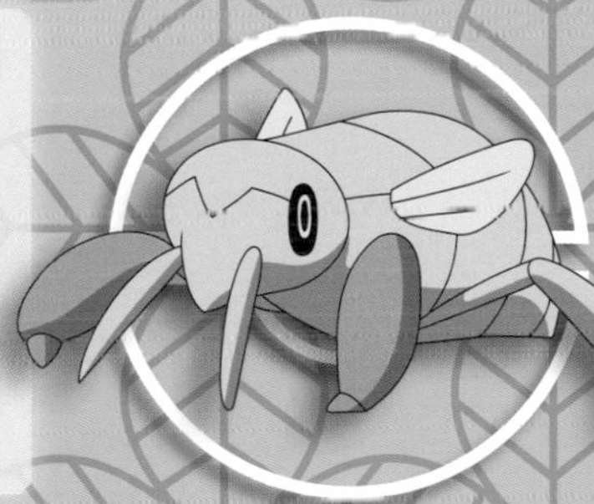

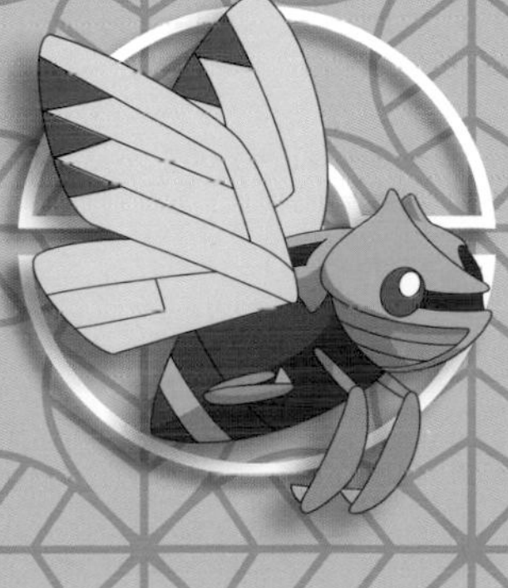

CATEGORY:
NINJA POKÉMON
TYPE: BUG-FLYING
HEIGHT: 2'07"
WEIGHT: 26.5 lbs
EVOLUTION:
Nincada ➛ **Ninjask** or Shedinja

NINJASK

At maximum speed, Ninjask flies so fast it's difficult to see. When it finds a tree with delicious sap, it gathers with others to nourish itself.

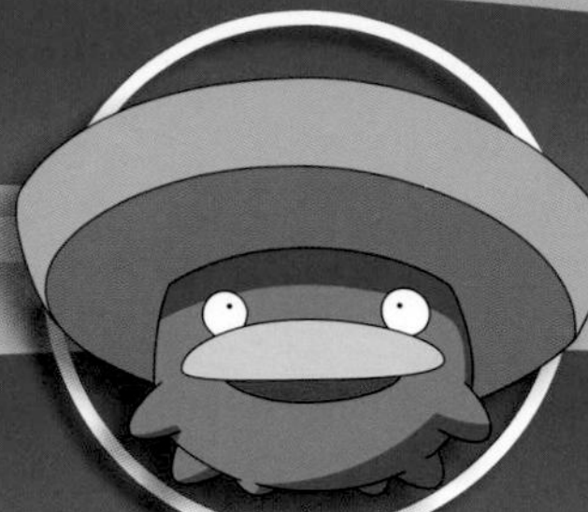

LOTAD

The large flat leaf that rests atop Lotad's head makes for an excellent means of travel across water for our smaller Pokémon friends.

CATEGORY:
WATER WEED POKÉMON
TYPE: WATER-GRASS
HEIGHT: 1'08"
WEIGHT: 5.7 lbs
EVOLUTION:
Lotad ➛ Lombre ➛ Ludicolo

TAILLOW

Taillow does not like the cold, and it flies up to 200 miles a day to find warmer habitats. In battle, it proves itself a true combatant, even in the face of its adversaries.

CATEGORY:
TINY SWALLOW POKÉMON
TYPE: NORMAL-FLYING
HEIGHT: 1'00"
WEIGHT: 5.1 lbs
EVOLUTION:
Taillow ➛ Swellow

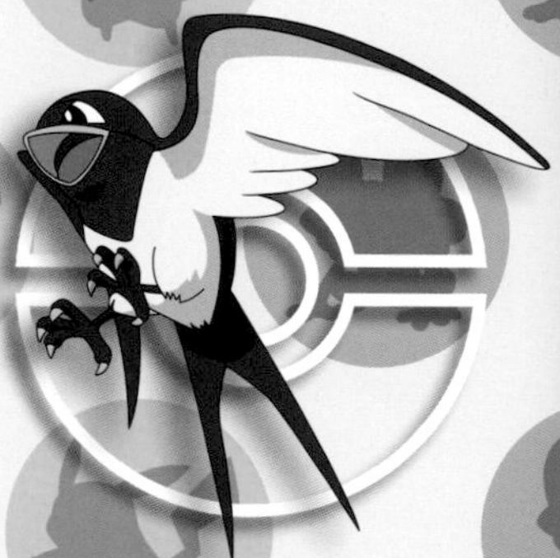

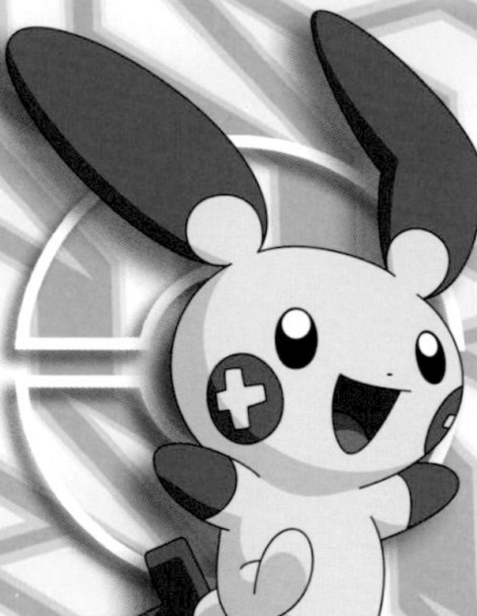

PLUSLE

Plusle loves to cheer for its fellow Pokémon. It creates sparkling pom-poms by shorting out the electrical current released from its palms.

CATEGORY:
CHEERING POKÉMON
TYPE: ELECTRIC
HEIGHT: 1'04"
WEIGHT: 9.3 lbs
EVOLUTION:
This Pokémon does not evolve.

TORCHIC

Thanks to the pocket of fire that burns eternally inside it, Torchic makes anyone who comes near it feel warm and comfortable. But beware! It isn't just cute and cuddly. Torchic can shoot fireballs at its enemies.

CATEGORY:
CHICK POKÉMON
TYPE: FIRE
HEIGHT: 1'04"
WEIGHT: 5.5 lbs
EVOLUTION:
Torchic ➛ Combusken ➛ Blaziken ➛ Mega Blaziken

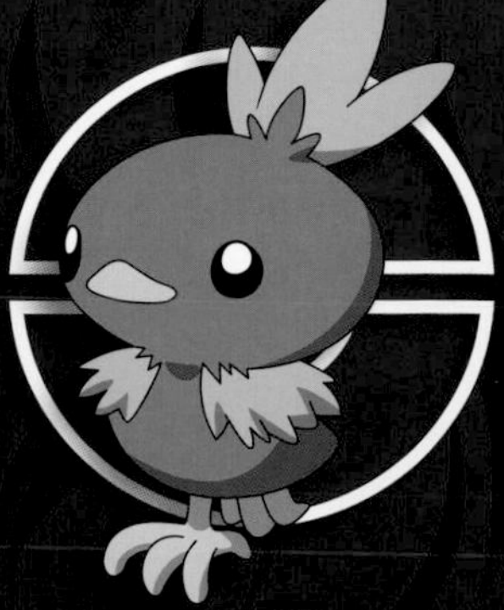

LOUDRED

Loudred's screams create sonic booms so powerful they can topple big trucks. When it starts stomping its feet, you know it's getting ready for combat.

CATEGORY:
BIG VOICE POKÉMON
TYPE: NORMAL
HEIGHT: 3'03"
WEIGHT: 89.3 lbs
EVOLUTION:
Whismur ➛ **Loudred** ➛ Exploud

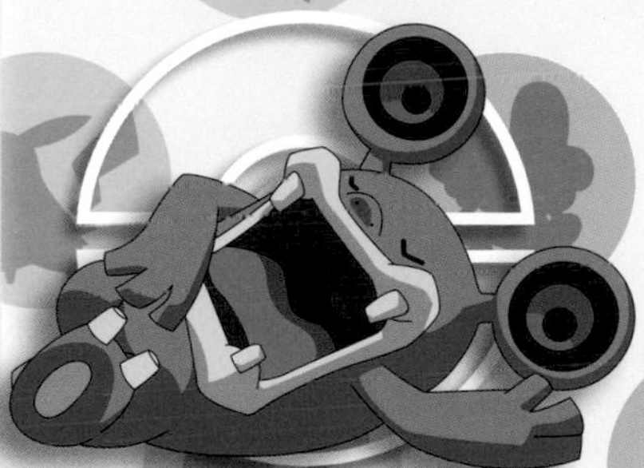

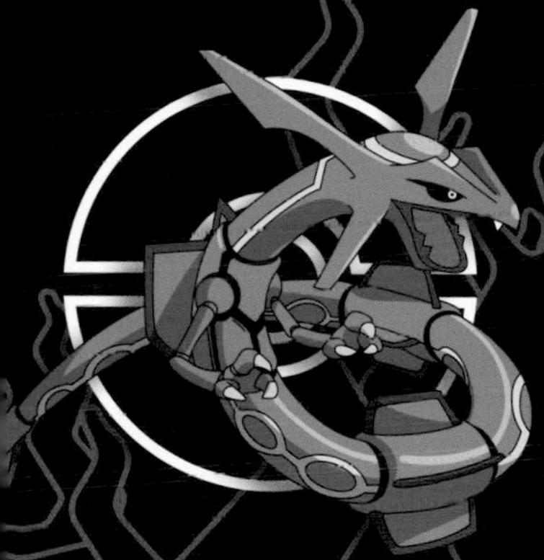

CATEGORY:
SKY HIGH POKÉMON
TYPE: DRAGON-FLYING
HEIGHT: 23'00"
WEIGHT: 455.2 lbs
EVOLUTION:
Rayquaza ➛ Mega Rayquaza

RAYQUAZA

Rayquaza lives in the ozone layer, above the clouds. This Pokémon is invisible from the ground.

REGICE

They say Regice was asleep inside a glacier for hundreds of years. Its body is made of ice dating back to the Ice Age.

CATEGORY:
ICEBERG POKÉMON
TYPE: ICE
HEIGHT: 5'11"
WEIGHT: 385.8 lbs
EVOLUTION:
This Pokémon does not evolve.

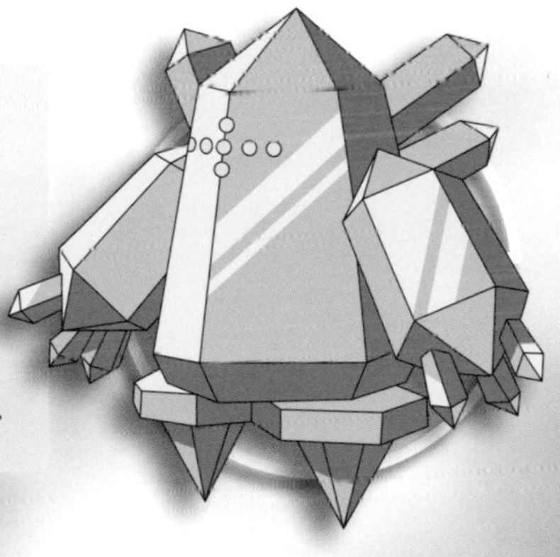

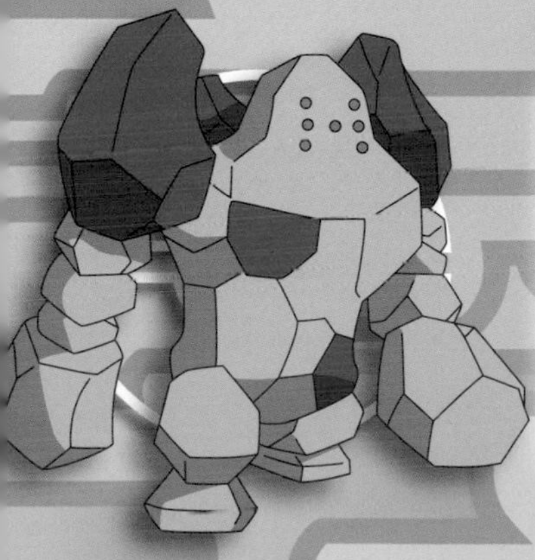

CATEGORY:
ROCK PEAK POKÉMON
TYPE: ROCK
HEIGHT: 5'07"
WEIGHT: 507.1 lbs
EVOLUTION:
This Pokémon does not evolve.

REGIROCK

Regirock is made entirely of rocks from different regions of the world. After combat, it repairs its damaged parts with stones.

REGISTEEL

Registeel's body is harder than any other metal. It is said that it was forged by subterranean pressure over tens of thousands of years.

CATEGORY:
IRON POKÉMON
TYPE: STEEL
HEIGHT: 6'03"
WEIGHT: 451.9 lbs
EVOLUTION:
This Pokémon does not evolve.

SABLEYE

Sableye lives inside caves and eats so many precious stones that its eyes have turned into gems! You can see its eyes glitter in the darkness.

CATEGORY:
DARKNESS POKÉMON
TYPE: DARK-GHOST
HEIGHT: 1'08"
WEIGHT: 24.3 lbs
EVOLUTION:
Sableye ➛ Mega Sableye

WAILMER

Wailmer plays by filling its body with water and bouncing around on the beach The more water it takes in, the higher it can jump. It sprays seawater out of the nostrils above its eyes.

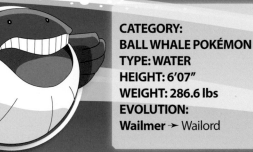

CATEGORY:
BALL WHALE POKÉMON
TYPE: WATER
HEIGHT: 6'07"
WEIGHT: 286.6 lbs
EVOLUTION:
Wailmer ➛ Wailord

WAILORD

When Wailord leaps from the water and lands on the surface, the shock wave is sometimes so intense it's enough to knock out its opponent.

CATEGORY:
FLOAT WHALE POKÉMON
TYPE: WATER
HEIGHT: 47'07"
WEIGHT: 877.4 lbs
EVOLUTION:
Wailmer ➛ **Wailord**

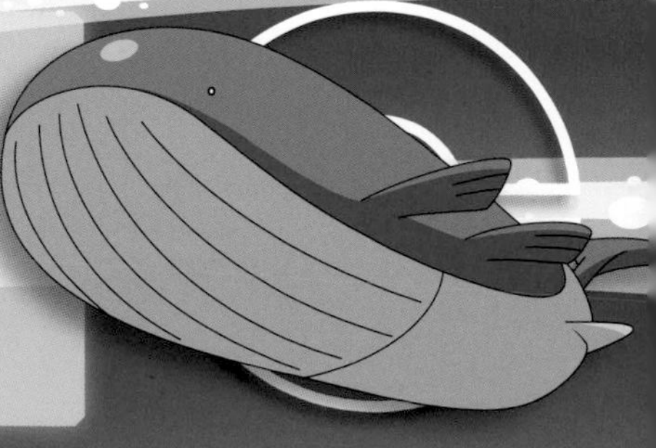